They were there when...

GOSPEL CHARACTERS REFLECT

Learn from the past,
Live in the present,
Believe in the future.

They were there when...

GOSPEL CHARACTERS REFLECT

Paul Bowes

Illustrations by Paul Gustave Doré

Published by Book Castle Publishing August 2022
ISBN 978 1 906632 18 2
Printed in Great Britain by TJ Books Ltd
Designed by Tracey and Steve Moren at Moren Associates Ltd

Dedicated
to my wife Ann, whose intrinsic Spirit shines out bright
to our children and grandchildren, inheritors of that light

Contents

INTROIT ix

INTRODUCTION xi

PREFACE xiii

THE ANGEL GABRIEL CAME DOWN… 1

Birth angel… 3
Zechariah, a Temple priest

The young mother-to-be… 7
Mary, the mother of Jesus

O LITTLE TOWN OF BETHLEHEM… 11

In a manger… 13
Joseph, the 'earthly' father of Jesus

First at the birth… 16
Bethlehem shepherd boy

Following yonder star… 19
Melchior, a Magus

Lying low… 22
Joseph, the 'earthly' father of Jesus

Paternal descent… 26
Talking Point

FRIENDS OF MINE, AND BROTHERS THROUGH LOVE...   27

The dove...   29
John the Baptist

The wilderness test...   34
Jesus

At the lake...   38
John, a disciple of Jesus

A challenge...   44
Andrew, a disciple of Jesus

The first shall be last...   48
Thaddeus, a disciple of Jesus

Feeding crowds...   52
A Galilean shepherd

BROTHER, SISTER, LET ME SERVE YOU...   55

Caught in the act...   57
Woman caught in adultery

Unclean...   61
A grateful leper

Dead or alive...   64
Jairus, a synagogue leader

Down among the demons...   68
Legion, a demoniac

Up a fig tree...   71
Zacchaeus, a tax collector

Water at the well...   74
Photine, a Samaritan woman

Pool...   77
Simon the Zealot, a disciple of Jesus

A healing ministry...   80
Talking Point

LORD, TEACH US...   81

Parables in brief...   83

OFT IN DANGER, OFT IN WOE...   93

Three siblings...   95
Lazarus, a friend of Jesus

The Law...   99
A strict Pharisee

The servant king...   103
Philip, a disciple of Jesus

Pieces of silver...   108
Judas Iscariot, a disciple of Jesus

Innocent...   112
Pontius Pilate, governor of Judaea

A burden shared...   118
Simon of Cyrene

Three times...   123
Simon Peter, a disciple of Jesus

HERE HANGS A MAN DISCARDED…   129

Suppression…   131
Roman soldier at the crucifixion

Penitence…   136
An observer of the crucifixion

Another beloved disciple?…   140
Mary Magdalene, a follower of Jesus

WE GIVE IMMORTAL PRAISE…   145

Only a mother…   147
Mary, the mother of Jesus

Seven miles home…   152
Cleopas, the uncle of Jesus

Wounds…   155
Thomas, a disciple of Jesus

Aftermath
YE CHOIRS OF NEW JERUSALEM…   159

Feasting and fasting…   161
Reuben, a devout Jew

…from your Valentinus…   165
Asterius, a Roman jailer

ABOUT THE ILLUSTRATOR/ABOUT THE AUTHOR   168

Introit

'Tell me, what did the booksellers think of my offerings this month?' would enquire Lady Collins of even the newest of London sales representatives - myself - in the office at the end of the day. 'How well are they selling?' A devout convert to Catholicism, yet the most ecumenical of publishers, she was justifiably proud of the prestigious, if eclectic, religious imprint she was so creatively compiling. The ethos might encompass academic brilliance from Ninian Smart, controversial theology from Hans Kung, 'plain man's' guidance from William Barclay, inspiration from C. S. Lewis at peak fame, individualistic ruminating from Malcolm Muggeridge, or an idiosyncratic 'Gospel according to Peanuts', as well as her championing of the Good News Bible in modern English. So she was not simply interested in the reaction of Hatchards or Foyles or the top religious bookshops. Equally important to her would be her books' reception in W H Smith's or by small independents or in department stores or on the mainline station bookstalls.

Of course, this universal access to the general book trade of the early Seventies owed much to its being repped alongside the rest of the fantastic Fontana paperbacks imprint under the stewardship of her younger son, Mark. He took the cream of his father Sir William Collins' suite of bestselling hardback authors and series and added original academic titles, along with the most popular children's authors in Armada and prestigious contributors to the related Lions imprint. An exciting era for the affordability and variety of books as the whole sector was expanding rapidly. And it heralded a golden age for the mass penetration of religious titles to every corner of the retail market throughout the country.

One particular author of hers, I remember, excited the whole publishing company at the time, myself included. An English Jew who used his unique gifts to enhance the penetration of the Bible's message, both via TV and in print. Principally via his 'Bible Stories' and 'The Book of Witnesses', allying an instinctive cultural empathy with fantastic storytelling gifts to present the drama of those far off times to a modern audience. The magic of the inimitable David Kossoff.

No doubt their influence on my subconscious has lingered silently there for the half a century since my impressionable early days in publishing and throughput my chequered history as a humble lifelong churchgoer. Because recently I was invited to compile one or two short contributions to both a Nonconformist church magazine and an Anglican village publication. Without really intending it, I found myself following loosely in those august footsteps, though without his intrinsic advantages and with only a conventional Christian heritage and understanding on which to draw. So their tone and emphasis inevitably contrasted markedly with his. Moving house to another area soon after, however, put a stop to those public offerings but I quietly continued to compile other imaginings in the same vein, though narrowing my scope just to the period covered by the Gospel story itself. Taking shape surreptitiously, I realised, was my life of Jesus as experienced by a few of those who were there when…

Introduction

Two millennia ago lived a man unique in history. Born into circumstances quite unpromising for prospering his predestined message of salvation for humankind. As he would doubtless have realised, his seed was to be sown in very rocky ground. Amongst humble rural folk in a lowly backwater province of the Roman Empire...Galileans looked down upon even by many of their fellow Jews...yet the whole nation was united in an inherited faithfulness to their one true God. Which put their religion at odds with worship practised by all other rival nations who revered a plurality of divine and semi-divine figures. And had long developed a rich well-established mythology around them.

Jesus was an erudite man, of good pedigree, some say noble, steeped in the religious laws and practices of his ancestors, then exploring and expounding that faith for years in his local synagogue settings. But with an unusually free-thinking approach, doubtless even at that stage stirring up unease amongst the hierarchy. Then in his maturity finally embarking on a three year crusade, but not in the style many of his contemporaries had been hoping for - as a Messiah who would throw off the Roman yoke. Instead, he lived out a mission from his God that defied logic and eventually transcended his own savage earthly death on a cross. Subsequently, his followers, inspired by an unshakeable conviction that he had been resurrected from his earthly tomb, established a tradition that in due course changed the world. Though not without much debate in the two millennia since, with theologians arguing, interpreting and moulding various nuanced insights and doctrines about those long ago happenings.

Hindsight may imply the inevitability of the unfolding outcome, belying its unlikely genesis in that chaotic period of history when Jewish leaders and Roman authorities were determinedly trying to keep the lid on any potential powder keg of societal dissent. The effect of this recurs constantly throughout Jesus's earthly years.

But his mission did not just encounter problems from his enemies. His own entourage failed to provide him with consistent support. Even the most passionate and empathetic were often confused. Indeed, even the gospels betray numerous accounts of his baffled parents and uncomprehending disciples.

That is hardly surprising. The contemporaries of Jesus, whether for or against or neutral, were coming to terms with an unprecedented situation. Challenged by his claims that often felt preposterous. Forced to react spontaneously to fast moving events. Being human confronting the divine. Living contemporaneously with Jesus, none could be expected to foresee where the future was heading, let alone how events would evolve around traditional Judaism…or the birth of Christianity.

Preface

Matthew, Mark, Luke and John. Four windows through which to view the life of Jesus on earth. Each gospel nuanced for a specific target audience. Accounts which may overlap, or even sometimes contradict. Not contemporary writings but based partly maybe on oral memories handed down for a generation or two, and then heavily interpreted through the Hebrew scriptures. By then, also influenced by the evolving political, social and religious backgrounds amongst which Jesus's teachings had begun to be spread, with Jews and Gentiles increasingly mingling around them.

Even the first gospel, probably Mark, was only written after Paul had begun his missionary work, had exerted an influence and had already written seven of his letters. The gospels were not the source of early Christianity, but its product, compiled from within existing Christian communities.

So, the white heat of the moment was tempered in the process of compiling the original gospels. Though the unfolding events are often dramatic, spontaneity is not the prime focus, intention or effect. Hindsight's influence is frequently evident. One can only speculate on how those mere mortals in the stories would have recounted them at the time. Baffled, impressed, shaken, uplifted, transformed, and subjected to many other human reactions as their lives were impacted by this charismatic man.

So, the Bible creates and tells their stories mostly in the third person, many years later. But how might a version written immediately in the first person have differed? Here is a collection of vignettes in that vein, featuring both major, minor and imaginary characters. Speculative elaborations, different emphases, controversial interpretations… integrated into this version of a gospel of witnesses. And remember… if the language occasionally sounds a little 'modern', think of it as a 'translation' from the original!

I wonder…what was it like to be there when…?

═══════════Footnote═══════════

Some bibles emphasise the 'words of Christ', especially in John's gospel, by printing them in red rather than black type. In fact, even allowing for any oral tradition, few attributions are likely to be truly verbatim. Instead, they are re-creations of Jesus's teaching style combined with Old Testament predictions and a doctrinal message, cleverly composed years later to help establish a foundation for a new faith developing among diaspora Jews and Gentiles in an ever-widening area far beyond the narrow homeland to which Jesus himself preached and taught.

THE ANGEL GABRIEL
CAME DOWN...

Birth angel...

Angels have often appeared to our Jewish ancestors, but I would never have considered myself sufficiently worthy to receive a personal message from one of God's messengers. But after a lifetime in his service, just such an encounter with an angel has brought me a harbinger of future personal glory. The mystery of it all is still unravelling, but so far...

It had always been a huge sadness, indeed shame, to me that my wife Elizabeth had been denied conception throughout our long devoted marriage. 'Is that somehow a sign of the Lord's displeasure with us, do you think, Zechariah?' she would occasionally ask me. The puzzling issue never threatened the faithful fulfilment of my priestly duties in the Temple, but I craved an answer. Though at my advanced age I had almost given up expecting one, however hard I prayed. And then the Lord blessed us. 'I can hardly believe this will finally be happening,' said a mystified, if excited, Elizabeth. 'Do you think he has some special purpose for us?' she continued, when eventually, in confused silent gesturing, I managed to convey what had been imparted to me.

I had been burning incense in the Temple sanctuary, that most coveted of all my duties. While everyone else stayed outside. A huge honour, already making the day very special for me. I was feeling very close to God as I closed my eyes in prayer. Then, terrifyingly, the Angel Gabriel suddenly appeared over to my right, explained his message, before, in rebuke at my incredulity, striking me dumb for the duration of her pregnancy. Such a life-changing turn of events. He brought instructions and news of a son he insisted we must name John, divinely destined to prepare multitudes to receive the Lord! 'A great man in God's sight… filled with the Holy Spirit from his mother's womb,' the angel promised. How tricky it was to convey all that to Elizabeth, or anyone, in my new dumb state. She and I will not live to see that mission fulfilled by our offspring but what a blessing for us to receive God's favour so very late in life! As a result, whilst waiting on God had been a familiar privilege, I now faced a test to do so in a unique silence of glad adoration.

As if that wasn't overwhelming enough…a few months later, by which time we were finally coming to terms with our own shock, I was staggered again to learn that Gabriel had subsequently been sent to Nazareth on an even more sacred mission…to announce a second miraculous conception, this time not to an elderly woman but to the youngest of girls! None other than our very own cousin Mary - so inexperienced and newly betrothed. 'Let it happen to me as you have said,' she acceded.

'Sounds impossible, I know, but an angel has told me I have been chosen to conceive by the Holy Spirit and to bear a boy, Jesus, who will be revered as the Son of the Most High,' she explained in a fearful voice to her incredulous intended, Joseph…knowing he'd had no part to play as yet. A righteous man, thus totally discomfited, his reaction was understandably dark. Dismiss her quietly and totally? Try to accept her wonderment as true? He realised he needed time to absorb the ramifications.

My own angelic experience helps me to credit Mary, though obviously life had become tense for her. So, how appropriate that the short-term solution has been an extended visit by her to our house in the hills…a chance for the two women to compare the angel's visits and to mull over their similarly awesome dramas. And as a sign of their entwined experiences…immediately on Mary's arrival, Elizabeth actually felt the five-month old baby leap in her womb. So, for the last few weeks, the two mothers-to-be, though bizarrely at opposite ends of their life-span, have been pondering together what God might be holding in store for themselves and their very special sons. In my mute condition, of course, I can't really partake.

But, in my heart, I have been unable to stop brooding on everything from the male point of view too. Worrying what may happen when Joseph receives Mary back home soon. He is a deep thinker, a devout man, so I am sure he is praying fervently for guidance. And I have come to this conclusion. God will not be leaving him to tackle the situation without sufficient personal reassurance. His angelic messenger Gabriel's task would not exclude him. I am sure he will have been sent to visit Joseph as he tosses and turns in restless dreaming. To calm his disturbed mind and conscience as they wrestle to comprehend his future role in this unfolding divine plan. Till he comes to appreciate with wholehearted conviction how much Mary and Jesus need his steadfast loving support. As I will sustain Elizabeth and John till my final breath.

Extraordinary, as I imagine the imminent little babies, to think of the challenge they will face against a backdrop of hazardous uncertainty in such troubled times. But actually, why do I harbour doubts? Why is my faith so small? Growing up as contemporaries, those cousins will inspire each other…and eventually thousands from all around. In fact, there are no limits. From the seeds they will sow, I believe God's redeeming message will grow irresistibly through generations to come…and maybe, just maybe, be carried beyond these lands and outside the Jewish people. That's not what I have ever anticipated before, but why not? His angels have opened my mind to a new vision. In God's grace, the salvation of the whole world is possible…indeed, inevitable.

Zechariah, a Temple priest

Footnote

In Jewish culture and biblical stories, angels are supernatural messengers from God, possessing form but not substance, acting as forces of spiritual energy.

Mentioned 273 times in the Bible, yet maybe many a modern reader doesn't notice them.

So they remain today a huge challenge to Western understanding with its greater emphasis on science and materialism.

The young mother-to-be...

It was my most exciting day as a little girl in Sepphoris. The day I heard who my parents had negotiated to be my future husband. Around preliminary discussions over future dowry arrangements, they had agreed to my being chosen for Joseph, a rather older boy of my acquaintance, by his father, known to us after having supervised major building work locally, despite originating from an influential family in Bethlehem. I was reminded of the text, 'It is not good for a man to be alone. I will make a helper suitable for him'. Only seven, I didn't understand fully, but in Joseph's case that seemed to mean me. I never once thought of exercising my right to refuse him later. And I grew up increasingly accustomed to the prospect. Actually, for years nothing really changed. Like all our friends in a similar position, we both just went back to the day to day, in my case eventually as a handmaid in the Temple. I really did do my best to please the priests…and God. And in that way, the years passed happily as I awaited the time when I would 'come of age'.

So, joy. Soon after my thirteenth birthday, I was finally ready to embrace our betrothal. Amidst much celebration and a happy procession, our partnership was confirmed publicly. A bit confusing for us in our excitement, because I would be remaining in my father Joachim's house, and we were not going to live together for another year, but there would meanwhile be much to prepare. A place to live, and all the wedding garments, lamps and a myriad other arrangements. So I dreamed of the future as all teenage girls do, whilst still carrying out my sacred Temple duties.

Certainly not anticipating what came next. I was just sitting quietly, deep in thought, when I felt a strange presence. A real shock at first. In a moment of sheer terror for me, an angel of the Lord appeared. 'Fear not,' he said soothingly. I would conceive a son by the Holy Spirit, I was told. King of the house of David, a descendant so long promised who would reign for ever. Blessed above all women, I would be. At my tender age! But I accepted in obedient humility, the Lord's servant-girl. A song of

praise burst from my heart and soul. Too much to take in really. Even my mother couldn't really help me later to make sense of it all.

Whatever would Joseph think? Disaster loomed. Inevitably, he would consider divorcing me quietly to avoid the shame, I reasoned in panic. I explained it all to him as best I could. A worthy young man, he took it hard. Worrying about the strict rules around adultery, including death by stoning. We discussed it further, urgently, but without any firm conclusions. On the precipice, it felt. How ironic the Proverb sounded, 'He who finds a wife finds what is good and receives favour from the Lord'. Almost too much favour around, I reckoned, with a wry smile.

It was decided I should visit my much loved cousin, Elizabeth, for a few months. She was five months pregnant, so I might be able to help her. Hopefully, eventually Joseph would come to me with quite a different attitude. An angel of the Lord might appear to him too, in a dream. 'Do not be afraid to take Mary as your wife!' he might hear, in reassurance. Our betrothal would continue. Despite the complications caused as my pregnancy would gradually become more and more obvious to all.

And so it came to pass. Inevitably, though, our marriage feast and festivities were somewhat compromised. But my beloved Joseph was determined to show his commitment to me before the birth. He brought the wedding formalities forward, in respect for me. But despite days of gaiety and excitement, including the traditional colourful procession into Joseph's house, it all wasn't quite what I had been envisaging... though I kept reminding myself that I had been so blessed by the Lord. That visit to Elizabeth had brought much reassurance. My baby would indeed be very special.

Our parents were confused too, of course. But I shall be eternally grateful that they put our wishes and feelings above their own doubts. I shared some more very moving moments with my wise mother, Anne. Much was being asked of us all. And in a further change from custom, my ever-supportive Joseph and I made another hard personal decision in agreeing to delay consummation until after the birth.

And that stage was to be even more bizarre. My delivery was imminent at just the wrong time. We needed to undertake the long, long journey to Bethlehem for census reasons beyond our control. So uncomfortable, so tiring. And when we finally reached our destination, there was no proper accommodation available. The last straw. I didn't feel in the least 'specially chosen'. It just felt cruel.

Mary, the mother of Jesus

Footnote

Today, Jewish girls are considered minors from the age of three to twelve; a young woman for six months after their first period; an adult thereafter. Maturity is regarded legally as beginning for girls at twelve years and a day, the earliest possible age of the very young Mary at her Annunciation experience, though neither her age nor Joseph's is known.

Nowadays, Orthodox girls become bat mitzvahs (daughters subject to the law) at age 12, Reform Jewish and Conservative girls at age 13.

The male equivalent, bar mitzvah (son subject to the law), takes place at age 13, though this specific ceremony can only be traced back to the Middle Ages.

Under normal circumstances in New Testament times, although the bride-to-be knew to expect her groom to come for her after about a year, she did not know the exact day or hour. He could come earlier than anticipated, though usually it was the father of the groom who gave final approval for that.

Hippolytus of Thebes stated that Mary died in AD 41.

O LITTLE TOWN OF BETHLEHEM...

In a manger...

A son who would be given the throne of his father David and has been conceived by my dear betrothed Mary and the Holy Spirit, I pondered, on hearing the extraordinary news. It took a little while, but eventually the picture became clear to me. What a privilege! As a result, over many months I made adjustments in our lives to facilitate this awesome responsibility. Now, just when the baby was due, how ironic that I have had to bring her for census reasons to Bethlehem where people of my lineage had been ordered to gather. It has been a really stressful journey for her, all the way from Galilee. Four or five days of discomfort and fatigue, I fear, despite riding on a donkey.

And on arrival here, matters initially went from bad to worse. In a house near one of the inns, the first-floor guest room we had been hoping to use was full. So our only option was to sleep with the livestock, overnighting in an adjacent ground-floor cave. At least we would be warmer there and safer from theft. But not from interruption, as we were to discover.

What else inopportune could go wrong, I wondered? Of course...the baby demanding to be born! A few kindly folk came out in the night to help Mary, though I know she was very sad that her mother couldn't be with her for reassurance and to share this special time. So, in that very basic but tranquil setting, God's beautiful baby boy was safely delivered. I will never forget the look on Mary's face as he was passed up to lie on her breast, eager to nestle and suckle. That frail little body was then laid reverently onto straw, lying at peace in the animals' manger, wrapped in swaddling clothes. Now understandably exhausted, the angelic young girl nevertheless looked totally contented. I gazed fondly on her, elated for us all. Now for some well-earned rest, I promised. But no!

Suddenly, in burst a group of excited young shepherds, having been kept awake on the nearby hillside in wondrous expectation under a particularly bright night sky. They had spotted our activity, had come to investigate and were thrilled to get the first chance to greet the new-born. Reminds us of one of our little lambs, they said. We feel so at home amongst the animals, they went on. Somehow, they added an authentic touch to the humble scene.

Then, a commotion outside. Travellers on camels this time. By complete contrast to the rest of the gathering, in walked three exotically dressed strangers who too had been attracted to our location by a bright starry sky…one star in particular that they had been tracking for hundreds of miles. Magi, pursuing a dramatic royal event. Marking their auspicious journey's end with precious gifts for the baby, of gold, frankincense and myrrh. In my mind flashed more thoughts of that throne of David prophecy. And then alarm bells rang when they confessed they had been consulting nearby Herod on the way here. In no sense would he be relaxed about any more rumours or on hearing any of the further details he had requested from them. Our visitors would realise that, I felt sure. And not risk jeopardising our vulnerable situation by meeting him again.

In due course, all our awesome visitors had said their reluctant farewells. Time finally, at the end of a quite extraordinary night for Mary and the infant - whom we had been told to name Jesus, meaning 'God is salvation' - to seek some long-overdue sleep. Me too.

Joseph, the 'earthly' father of Jesus

Footnote

This is one possible merger of the gospel accounts, which are actually irreconcilable in detail. The traditional nativity story combines elements of legend, prophecy, history, theology, scripture, ancestry etc which all conflict.

For example, all the dates around Augustus Caesar's census, Herod the Great, Archelaus, Cyrenius etc do not tie up. Likewise the possible 'star' explanations.

In particular too, the link to Bethlehem is tenuous. Though Joseph may actually have had relatives there. Jews would not normally stay at an inn, as the food wasn't kosher and Jews were not allowed to eat with other Roman or foreign travellers.

Local sheep were not hardy enough to be outdoors overnight in the two or three winter months, only from March to November.

Even the details of the connections with Nazareth are not fully agreed by modern scholars.

The now traditional Christmas Day replaced the Roman mid-winter festival of the 'Unconquerable Sun' on December 25th.

First at the birth...

Even now I can't really believe it all happened. See what you think.

Let me introduce myself. My name is Abraham, a proud traditional Jewish shepherd's name. My father, a priest shepherd, chose it, knowing I would be following in his footsteps tending the special sheep around the Magdal Eder, a tower about a mile east of Bethlehem. From there you can certainly 'watch over the flocks by night', that most dangerous of times for our profession, as you can imagine.

We shepherds don't just graze and water the sheep, and shear them and milk them. We also have to protect them from shady thieves and predatory animals. Sheep really would be helpless at times without us. I'm only a teenager but I take my responsibilities seriously. You see, our sheep are not like the normal ones kept out in the wilderness areas. They are much more precious. The best of them, the perfect specimens, are intended for sacrifice in the Temple here. Sometimes we even have to wrap the tiny newborn in swaddling cloths in a manger.

Many a night my friends and I have spent in the cold, in the dark, in the fields with our sheep. Bit monotonous sometimes, but I do love the chance to meditate quietly in communion with God in prayer. But I never expected to be a special part of his plan for mankind. Bizarre experience, I can tell you.

Possibly my eyelids had been drooping, but suddenly the sky lit up. The dazzle of not just one angel, but a multitude. Terrifying. But then,

oh that glorious singing about peace and goodwill. And, best of all, the news of a Saviour just born in David's city. Why ever were we common shepherds being treated to such an extraordinary announcement? And then I suddenly thought of one of our little sacrificial lambs. And I tucked him under my arm to take to show to the new baby boy...as I was to discover, in his own manger, no less.

A few friends and I dashed off down the hill. And we found him in a sort of cave shelter behind an inn, surrounded by animals. His mother was very gentle, but oh so young. How touched we were to feel her sublime presence. And the older man with her was so caring towards them both. A simple carpenter by trade apparently, he told us. They too had been visited by angels a while ago, explaining how uniquely chosen and favoured they were to nurture this newborn...the lamb of God, you might say. So likewise, we shepherds were awestruck to be a humble part of this cataclysmic event. Though baffled when three much posher visitors and their entourage appeared on the scene!

Glory and praise to God...out we went with a vow to spread the wonderful news to all we might meet. That baby was destined to change the world, we knew for certain. And I wouldn't be surprised if he grew up to become the ultimate 'good shepherd'. Not a bad job to have, you know!

Bethlehem shepherd boy

Footnote

A classic example of the divine and the everyday blending seamlessly. What a wonderful lesson in humility that God's son should be born in a cave/stable where the first visitors were mere shepherds, called by the angels to interrupt their mundane routine hillside occupation and celebrate under a star.

Following yonder star...

My duties as a Zoroastrian priest are normally very strict and routine. After all, our Persian power is renowned for its disciplined ways. But just occasionally I am involved in something out of the ordinary, and one of the most remarkable such undertakings took me on a journey hundreds of miles to the west, I recall.

Our religion has an international reputation for its meticulous astronomical record-keeping. Century after century. So much so, that, through spotting any irregular movements of the stars, we are perfectly placed to perceive meanings hidden from others. On that particular occasion we observed an unusually bright object in the skies. Trawling through international records for its possible significance, I found a prediction that it might be heralding the birth of a ruler. And as I watched it moving slowly westwards, I pondered on a Jewish prophecy in Micah, 'Bethlehem, you are one of the smallest towns in Judah, but out of you I will bring a ruler for Israel, whose family line goes back to ancient times'. It intrigued me especially to think

that their God would choose to use the humblest of places for such a major event. Much to investigate, I thought, and I reckoned that a couple of other magi that I knew well, Caspar and Balthazar, might wish to join me, Melchior, on such a quest. We all gathered in Saba, with an entourage, and fully provisioned for a long ride. For their endurance, relying on our trusty camels, rather than our fine Arabian horses.

Weeks later, following the path of the star throughout, we neared our likely destination. A new ruler, we thought? So surely it makes sense to call on the local King Herod in Jerusalem. Only protocol, after all. But he was furious. Knew nothing about it. Didn't believe a word. Then... 'perhaps you could locate it more precisely and let me know, please?' We promised to try, but started to worry what might transpire if we did.

Initially, no immediate surprise. The star did indeed seem to dwell finally over Bethlehem. Such a busy town that night but we tracked down some activity behind one of the inns. And in a stable/cave we found the most touching of scenes. Lowly animals, some naive shepherd boys, a local couple quietly helping, an adoring husband, a very young mother and a new born boy, wrapped in swaddling clothes and lying in a straw-filled manger. Appropriately, the sort of humility we had anticipated. Strange people, those Jews! Anyway, time for us to pay homage.

We knew that typical Jewish offerings might have been a sheep or a calf. But we had brought far more appropriate gifts. Valuable gold to represent royalty and virtue; divine frankincense to represent worship and prayer; embalming myrrh to represent

persecution, suffering and death. A wonderful outcome to our quest and far more thought-provoking even than we had expected.

No way would we unleash mighty Herod's intrusion on such a family, whatever his wrath with us. Our mission was accomplished. It now demanded a swift start to our return journey...by a different route. Back home to study the heavens again...with much learned.

Melchior, a Magus

Footnote

Nothing in Matthew identifies the priests as kings or rulers of any kind. The tradition, including the camels, is mostly an extrapolation from several Old Testament prophecies. Even there being three Magi is only based on there being three gifts.

Marco Polo in the thirteenth century reported on three large and beautiful tombs in Saba, the bodies still entire, with hair and beard remaining. However, a shrine in Cologne cathedral purports to have held their bones since the twelfth century. Archetypal conflicting medieval relic claims.

Not surprisingly, the Magi are some of the patron saints of travellers.

Modern astronomy can find no convincing evidence for a star around the appropriate dates. Not a supernova, not a comet, not a meteor, not a solar flare, not a great conjunction or planetary alignment of, say, Jupiter and Saturn or Venus.

Lying low...

In the last year or two, a few of my friends have most movingly explained their initial reaction on seeing their first-born. 'Life will never be the same' being the universal message. Too right. In my case too, on top of that human reaction, I am having to process a complicated new relationship with God involving my beloved Mary. In recent weeks, however, she and I have begun to feel a whole new purpose for our lives as we gaze at the tiny infant whose upbringing we must oversee.

Having moved out of the Bethlehem stable where he was born on that confusing if momentous night, we have been grateful to those who have since rallied round to support us. We are amongst friends here, but far from home. Unfortunately, however, I haven't been able to shake off a sense of imminent danger threatening my precious family. From Herod's thirst for revenge mainly, even if those influential visitors from afar did indeed avoid updating him on our whereabouts. The earlier assertions of such high-profile wise men will have sufficiently convinced him that a mysterious threat to his throne could have been born locally, so we needed to avoid any search parties he might organise.

Before worrying unduly about that though, the usual crucial religious customs around our newborn had to be observed, whatever the risk. Firstly, Jesus's circumcision and naming after eight days by the local rabbi, once Mary had reached the end of her ceremonial impurity. Then, after remaining hidden for a further obligatory month, we could complete her full purification from childbirth, along with Jesus's consecration… though both would require a trip to the Temple in Jerusalem, the ultimate danger spot in terms of our possible detection by the authorities.

We had accordingly entered the city and the Temple precincts very circumspectly. The last thing we expected was to be noticed immediately, but soon we were marvelling all over again as our little bundle was greeted in awe by yet more complete strangers. Special ones too. Shepherds and foreigners in the stable had been surprising enough, but adulation by Jews at the Temple was quite another matter, I told myself. The unobtrusive simple sacrifice of two turtle doves in thanksgiving had been our principal intention. But suddenly a most devout old man asked quietly if he could hold the baby in his arms; then he prayed softly, 'Master, my eyes have seen your salvation, a light for the glory of both your people Israel and also the gentiles.' The whole world? Remarkable. He told Mary how blessed and challenged she would be in the years ahead. For my part, not being the true father, how reassuring it was to hear him recognise the week-old baby as God's unique son, just as had been foretold.

That's not all. Just as we were preparing to leave, it happened again! A very elderly woman approached - possibly a prophetess, I surmised. Because she burst forth in similar praise to God, vowing to tell everyone that Jesus would one day deliver his people. At that, all the prospective responsibility finally overwhelmed us. How could we ever do him justice? And, in the short term, how could we even manage to keep him safe? Rumours were spreading about Herod's rage.

That night, I wrestled with the problem, tossing and turning, at the mercy of a most traumatic dream. The obvious move would have been to return home now. But I awoke with a new resolution. My plan will be very arduous for Mary and the baby, I am all too aware, but she is a resilient teenager and Jesus has been thriving in his first few weeks.

And, as she has reminded me, God is always with us...literally, you could say! So, I will say it quickly...I am making hurried preparations to lead us immediately on another even longer journey, this time to lie low outside Herod's jurisdiction in Egypt, where there is a large Jewish community. Better safe than sorry, however stressful initially. The future of the world might depend on that baby, I was being told. Maybe it would even be advisable to wait there till Herod dies and only then go back to Galilee.

Joseph, the 'earthly' father of Jesus

Footnote

Hugely symbolic are those revelations to Simeon and Anna towards the end of their faithful lives in God's service.

The Nunc Dimittis (Song of Simeon) has been a revered blessing for believers ever since.

Such a journey to Egypt would have taken no less than three weeks to walk.

Messianic beliefs flourished at the time in Egypt where there were many Jewish philosophers and wise men.

In his attempt to kill Jesus, Herod ordered the execution of all male boys under the age of two in the vicinity of Jerusalem... known today as the Slaughter of the Innocents.

Talking Point

Paternal descent...

Traditionally, Joseph was on a royal lineage from King David of ancient Israel, though the list is incomplete after Jechonia (as condemned by Jeremiah). Genealogy via males (Matthew lists 40 male names from Abraham) was important to Jews, yet strangely Matthew also includes four related females, all 'suspect' as foreign, a seductress, adulterous, or a prostitute.

Ironically, that would have softened any possible accusations amongst contemporaries about Mary's 'questionable' pregnancy! Joseph, traditionally older than his betrothed, the very young Mary, needed to believe/accept she was pregnant via the Spirit, not by another human. (Actually, much contemporary Greco-Roman culture featured gods who similarly fathered offspring who were later exalted to a heavenly state of eternal grace.) Regardless, he had the difficult task of conquering not just his incomprehension but also the understandable emotions of possible betrayal, along with any legal threat. Of course, ironically a divine parentage also negates strict talk of Jesus being of Joseph's lineage anyway. In human terminology, illegitimate on the male line. Though there are suggestions that Jesus may also have been of royal/priestly descent via Mary (as in Luke).

Joseph's role in Jesus's upbringing seems minor, relatively short-lived, or at least minimally recorded. The village of Nazareth was small and humble, despite those royal connections/ aspirations. A mysterious paradox there? Occupation-wise, Roman work would have been available in nearby bustling Sepphoris and Tiberias, as Joseph was probably more a stonemason/builder than a modern-style carpenter. Probably Jesus helped him at work; alongside developing much literacy and learning (also at home?) via discussion in the synagogue. The temple story, when his parents 'mislaid' him amidst much incomprehension, is maybe an add-in to the Bible, though representative of his religious studying and his dawning realisation of his future destiny/fate.

How did Jesus handle having two 'fathers' as he grew up amongst a conventional Jewish family? Assuming that Joseph died in Jesus's youth, he could not have been a major sounding-board in discussing Jesus's divine pedigree and the mission for God and Israel. Maybe Jesus missed the benefit of his experience, and he was certainly not alive when Jesus came to fame alongside his cousin John. If Joseph actually died really early on, some scholars claim that complex clues suggest Mary might have followed custom in marrying Cleopas, his brother, in which case bearing some or all of her later six children by him.

Returning to how far Jesus fulfilled genealogical expectations, Hebrew prophets had long predicted a Messiah to lead Israel in the last days, still then expected at any time. Part political, part heaven on earth...not necessarily clear. But the subjugated people's ongoing unrest was a threat well known to the Herod family and to the Roman authorities alike. Many rebels had already been executed accordingly, including members of the Sanhedrin even. Joseph has no recorded influence on the politics, but there was a continuing feeling that someone soon (Jesus, his brothers, the wider family, John etc) might be the latest generation to try to re-establish that royal dynasty. One can only speculate on how much a longer-lived human father would have encouraged or been proud of Jesus's possible twin mission. Or, seeing the dangers that accompanied Jesus's popularity, might he have taken the other path - would he have been too wary to undertake any involvement in advancing his son's aims?

FRIENDS OF MINE, AND BROTHERS THROUGH LOVE...

The dove...

Such devout people, my parents, being of priestly stock. In awe of the Temple and all its traditions. Devoted their last years to ensuring my childhood was centred around a deep desire to do God's will, as they had themselves always aspired to do. In fact, they explained that, before my conception, an angel had foretold a special role for me when I grew up. They stressed that I must never partake of wine or strong drink, so as to remain pure in readiness for a holy lifestyle. In some ways, it was a little overwhelming. At other times, I found the prospects exciting. From time to time, whenever I met my cousin Jesus, I explored these feelings with him. The same age as me, he felt like a kindred spirit in every way. I sensed a special empathy and holiness in him, even in those early days. Maybe our paths would cross in the future somehow, I wondered. Meanwhile, as I had been born so late on in my parents' lives, I felt they were never likely to nurture me beyond the verge of maturity.

So, when they died I felt a responsibility to honour their expectations of me. However, I had latterly grown very concerned about the way the Jewish priesthood was being drawn into politics and collaboration with the Roman occupiers. No doubt they felt they were acting as the people's shield, but God's will for us wasn't down that route, I was certain. Surely it was time to use my new independence and widen my experience. There were several other strands of Judaism to explore.

In particular, I knew that the desert harboured a community that had cut its ties with the secular world. Very anti the Temple of today, they had left Jerusalem to live in the wilderness near the Dead Sea, isolated from other Jews. To prepare the way of the Lord, following the commands of the prophet Isaiah. A sacred calling, awaiting better days when the Temple could be reconstituted with a purer style of priesthood. When they, the Sons of Light, would defeat the assorted Sons of Darkness and usher in a new kingdom of God.

I found these Essenes' entry rules very strict, insisting on obedience to the leadership and their overwhelmingly male monastic routines. But I warmed to their apocalyptic teachings of a kingly Messiah of David allied to a priestly Messiah of Aaron. And their search for an associated prophet figure seemed a sound proposition. Could that possibly be the role God intended for me? It was a challenging thought.

One memorable night, I felt God calling me to take a drastic change of direction again in his further service, to depart their formal ways and set off on a new quest, into the surrounding harsh landscape, and take a few others with me. A major break from all the security and peace of isolationism in order to confront the vagaries of the turbulent everyday world. A daunting upheaval, but we would put our trust in God. Perhaps the transformation was best symbolised by our having to exchange the cleanliness of our white robes in favour of the more practical attire of camel-hair tunics, girded by a leather belt. Clearly, asceticism comes in more than one guise. And we knew we would be relying in future on the uncertain generosity of others for food, if need be falling back on a diet such as wild locusts and honey.

For a while we prayed for guidance and reassurance, but there soon came proof that we should never have doubted God. Immediately we began our challenge, we encountered a welcome from so many folk in the local villages. In fact, several joined us on a permanent basis as additional disciples under my lead. But I never meant to wander around endlessly. I hoped for sufficient momentum, such that people would come to me. We were calling everyone we met to repentance of their sins as a first step to a new life. Offering the ritual of baptism, with which we were so accustomed, as its outward sign.

For that we needed a specific location. Eventually we located an ideal site in the lower Jordan valley where we could welcome everyone. At Al-Maghtas, enabling us to utilise some springs and pools too. And from miles around folk flocked there in droves. Obviously God was spreading the word, bringing them to me, his humble instrument. Where I would be inviting all to experience, not the familiar noise and bustle of the towns or the villages, or even the indoor surroundings of a synagogue, but a wholly respectful outdoor silence, leading to a sense of reverence which pervaded our moving ceremony, day after day. However, at first I had had to make some very firm warnings to ensure everyone would treat this opportunity with the utmost seriousness. 'You brood of vipers,' I admonished. 'Don't dare carry on being hypocritical or selfish. If you are not fruitful, God will cut you down and throw you into the fire. Be fair, be unselfish, be satisfied, don't be greedy. Turn over a new leaf now, or someone even more challenging than me may one day confront your inadequacies, with dire consequences.' My strictures hit home, preying on their conscience, such that they either slunk away or came meekly to repentance in the healing waters of my baptism. As a result, over time, hundreds and hundreds were genuinely finding their lives turned around. I thought I had thereby fulfilled God's expectations

of me, but no... In a split second I will never forget, his actual ultimate purpose for me became clear.

I definitely had an increasing feeling that God had chosen me to be a modern-day prophet, but I wondered how that could be. Now all was to be revealed. That day, I had already baptised dozens in an atmosphere somehow even more spiritual and obedient than usual. From my spot standing in the river, I looked up to greet the next in line. Unexpectedly, wading slowly towards me was my cousin, Jesus. All the way from his home in Galilee, I assumed, just to receive my blessing. I had a flashback to our childhood days. This must be the one! Without warning, I felt myself tremble. It seemed as if God himself was approaching. For this special man, I instinctively knew I was not sufficiently worthy. 'I need to be baptised by you, yet you have come to me,' I said, in a faltering voice. But he insisted. 'Let it be so. It is proper for us to do this to fulfil all righteousness.' So, with a deeper humility than I had ever known, I consented. I supported that body so tenderly as it slipped quietly down into the waters of baptism, and back upright. We looked deep into each other's eyes and then embraced for a moment, silently praying, both moved beyond further words. Quietly, he began to wade back to shore, and suddenly I sensed a spirit of peace like a dove descend on him. I heard a voice say, 'This is my beloved Son, with whom I am well pleased.' For sure, he had no need of my forgiveness of his sins...as there personified was the kingdom of God at hand.

I finally knew I had accomplished my role as God's essential prophet, as a forerunner with a unique destiny. In that water, I had stood on the threshold of a new era. I had held in my arms the man who would baptise with the Holy Spirit and with fire. Who would be the salvation of us all, showing mankind the way to God.

John the Baptist

Footnote

The Catholic Church commemorates John on two feast days. His nativity on June 24th, his beheading on August 29th.

In Eastern churches, every Tuesday throughout the year is dedicated to his memory, plus four further feast days.

Early Christian art depicts John as a tall, thin, gaunt, bearded figure. As an ascetic, bearing a staff, plus scroll/book/dish with a lamb inscription or motif.

On Jordan's Bank the Baptist's Cry...is a popular advent hymn by Charles Coffin.

In many Mediterranean countries the summer solstice is dedicated to St John.

John is the name-giving patron of the Knights Hospitaller.

The wilderness test...

The time has come.

I was sent to earth by the will of my Father. Tasked now to combine that divinity with my subsequent thirty years' experience of learned humanity. Steeped throughout in a Jewish heritage, made manifest in a unique people faithful to the Father, their one true God. So there is nowhere more appropriate as the foundation and platform for my task. Such a beacon of trust I must now rekindle, renew and set ablaze in an everlasting and universal fire.

Baptism recently in the sacred river by my cousin John has marked the turning point. Affirmed in that supreme moment by the Father's love and confidence in my resolve. Subsequently, I have been led by the Spirit into the desert. Withdrawing to pray and prepare. There continuing to commune with my loving Father whilst also facing an insidious attack from the evil one. Learning how to establish myself on the right path. To sort out my true priorities. In a cauldron of physical and spiritual stress, to anticipate the dilemmas ahead. Forty days of solitude among wild beasts, and with all the distracting and conflicting thoughts that even simply being in such an environment inevitably evokes. Beset at times by Satan's challenges to cope by abusing my potentialities. Feeling discomfited by some overwhelming temptations to stray away from my main focus, to succumb to selfish dreams and vanity.

Firstly, that crushing hunger, demanding relief from the all too human pangs of physical weakness being increasingly exacerbated by my extreme fasting in this barren landscape, away from everyday resources. Tempting me to misuse God-given powers that could turn the very stones at my feet into the nourishing bread that my body craves. But I have long learned that one is not sustained by bread alone but rather by the word and presence of God. Which I am here in the wilderness to be truly refreshed and nourished by.

Secondly, how could I speed up the impact of my future role? I am tempted to think...how much more effectively could I amaze the doubters by staging a spectacular event? Imagine the instant impact of throwing myself headlong from the highest parapet of the Temple, with the angels swooping down to save me. Awesome. Well, maybe dramatically effective, but unsound, unrealistic. That is not the way. It is not appropriate to test God in that fashion. Miracles are not just for show. They are for the selfless benefit of everyone.

Thirdly, nor is there any role for shallow shortcuts. Nor for the imposition of transformation through force, succumbing in obedience to the powers of darkness. The whole world instead needs to hear the word of God, implement it and change in his image. New standards are not achieved by conquest, but by setting a righteous example. By teaching humility, love, justice and peace. By worshipping and serving the Father.

When I leave this place, the way ahead will be hard. I am under no illusions. However well I lead, however well I teach, many will not comprehend, even my closest and dearest followers. The world today is full of cruelty, unfairness, inequality and corruption. In society, in politics, even in religion. Adversaries will abound.

However, after I leave, resourced by this prayerful solitude and emboldened to re-engage with the everyday, to embark humbly on a ministry to all around me, I will sow seeds that bear fruit not only in

the here and now but also in generations to come. The rest of my time on earth will be totally subject to the will of the Father. If necessary - and I fear, in this sinful world, it will be - even unto an atoning death, whatever form that may take.

But one promise is sure…in the fullness of his time we will all meet again in God's heaven.

Jesus

Footnote

In Luke, Jesus says he saw Satan fall 'like lightning from heaven'.

Satan, the sinful impulse, is the adversary who strives to test all God's servants, to prevent them from carrying out the divine will.

At the lake...

Nowhere could ever replace the Lake of Galilee in my affections as my favourite place. Of course, I inherited the passion for it from my father Zebedee, as he taught my elder brother James and me the subtle arts of being a fisherman there. And all the other fishermen form such a close-knit community, sharing even with a youngster like me ever more ways to harness all the appropriate techniques and elemental forces used to maximise a catch.

Imagine my surprise, then, that I have come to admire hugely an acquaintance without that background who at times can even beat us fishing experts at our own game, and in many other ways too. He had left his native Nazareth to work from a base in Capernaum, so he was just walking around the lake one day when he initially came across my friends Andrew and Simon who were as usual casting their nets from the shallows by the shore, then pulling them back in with the attached long rope. They were hoping to exploit a particular spring of clear warm water where vast shoals gather from time to time, but on that occasion maybe they were fed up at being particularly unlucky. Or simply bowled over by their unexpected visitor. Anyway, in no time they had suddenly agreed to leave their nets with the hired hands and follow him around in future in support of his nascent itinerant cause.

My brother James and I were nearby, in the boat mending our nets, so he approached us next. In a few minutes this inspirational figure changed our lives, inspiring us to join him too. I will never forget his choice of words which we found irresistible...'Come after me and I will make you fishers of men.' And his promises have come true. Not only in attracting more disciples and regular followers, but also hundreds of others have flocked to hear him or be healed by him. This Jesus has made us famous for miles around.

Actually, the Lake of Galilee has formed the backdrop to many amazing incidents and much of our activity together. Lots of gatherings on the shore and on nearby slopes, often lasting so long that they lead to spectacular feeding issues on occasion. Sometimes Jesus was even forced to resort to preaching from a boat if the press got too intense.

After one such occasion he suggested that Simon should take the fishing boat out a little further in pursuit of a catch. A couple of other boats followed suit. Not surprisingly, all of us fellow fishermen were a bit sceptical about his request. During the night before, we had been fishing as usual with the long drag net. Despite our oft-proven tactics of illumination by flares of oiled rag in the iron cage at the bow, accompanied by the noise of old metal cans being beaten together to drive the fish towards the net...no success. A daytime attempt now, without such aids, surely stood no chance. Normally. But we experts obeyed his instructions. And despite having laboured all night for nothing, we immediately found ourselves in the midst of a vast shoal of fish, so that the overfull nets were broken in pulling them all in. Notwithstanding, the haul filled two boats and nearly sank them.

You would have thought that Simon in particular had learned

the lesson to have faith in Jesus's instructions. But another incident makes one wonder. We had all had an exhausting day with a large crowd near the lake. So much so, that he sent us all off on the boat back to Capernaum while he stayed behind in peace to rest and pray. Unfortunately, conditions hampered us as we struggled to make headway on the lake. Then we suddenly saw him walking towards us on the water. Impetuous Simon got worried for his safety and jumped overboard, intending to help. However, thereby getting into trouble himself. So the rescue attempt had to be reversed! 'Oh you of little faith, why did you doubt?' he admonished. At once, weather conditions improved and progress resumed normally. So impressed were we that the realisation went round, 'Of a truth, you are the Son of God.'

When I reflect, Jesus's control of the elements shouldn't really have surprised us. An earlier incident also put us seasoned sailors to shame. On that occasion Jesus had been recuperating on one of the boats whilst we were crossing the lake. Not untypically, there came the sound of distant thunder, then heavy black masses of cloud rolled down the hills, lifting the hitherto placid waters into an angry sheet of foam, threatening to sweep over the boat. We were alarmed, and it takes a severe lashing to provoke our concerns. For peace and quiet, meanwhile, Jesus had been in the boat's little cabin at the stern, resting his head on the hard, stuffed leather roll we use as a pillow. The commotion outside never touched him. Simply stood up and said, 'Be quiet, be still,' and in no time the winds dropped, the clouds disappeared, and the lake returned to perfect calm. Local conditions allow for that transformation sometimes, but the apparent instant reaction of the elements to his air of authority was remarkable.

Jesus has transformed the whole atmosphere amongst the people living around the lake, and in Galilee generally. For the wider world I have great expectations too. Personally, Jesus has become not only a

leader but also a very special friend, despite my tender years. He often talks to us privately to explain his hopes for the future - some incredibly tricky and dangerous. But, whatever happens, I vow to stay alongside him to the very end.

John, a disciple of Jesus

Footnote

For their zeal James and John were called 'Boanerges' or 'sons of thunder' by Jesus.

John is a central figure in Christian teaching - possibly the beloved disciple who stood by the cross, comforting Mary.

He became one of the pillars of the Jerusalem church after Jesus's death. Traditionally thought to have lived to a very old age, possibly being buried at Ephesus.

A Challenge...

Whatever have we let ourselves in for! One moment my brother Simon and I were planning a routine catch in the lake, when a passer by accosted us. It was Jesus, whose cousin John I was involved with. Very persuasively he spoke, and once we realised that our friends, James and young John, would do likewise, we agreed to follow him. Nothing could have prepared us though for what quickly became our new daily routine. Day after day with him on whirlwind tours of Galilee and beyond.

At first we had to work hard to arouse people's interest, but soon our leader's remarkable reputation did that job for us. Proclaiming the good news of a different sort of kingdom, as well as treating the sick. In fact, soon so many flocked to us that we had difficulty maintaining order in the often desperate crush. Diseased, possessed, epileptic, paralysed… there seemed no one he couldn't put on the path to a better future. Almost overwhelmed though, eventually we needed a little respite up in the hills. I think he felt the pace might be getting too much for us. And maybe he worried not to have had enough time to tutor us. This was his chance. A few of us gathered round in more peaceful surroundings and listened attentively. In fact, however, before long the crowds caught up with us once more. He was inspired that day, and we were all treated to a series of lessons that could transform our lives.

Not surprisingly, perhaps, when you consider the range of disadvantaged folk we had mostly been encountering, it seemed that they were the focal point of his concerns. The poor, the gentle, the mourning, the hungry, the persecuted. Not only that, but as a consequence, the same humble people became the backbone of his support. And, as an aside, he warned every one of his followers never to be complacent, because the moment might well come when we would feel put upon for his sake. The high and mighty would stop at nothing to keep us in our place.

But the basic teaching went far beyond even that. Firstly, we must never cease striving to raise our own standards. Join him in setting an example to others. Be the salt of the earth, be a metaphorical light shining in the darkness. Maintaining the Law, certainly, but going further. Extreme rules obviously need obeying…of course no one should commit murder or adultery. But actually wrong thinking is just as bad. If you feel so tempted, come down hard on yourself before it's too late and you go even further off the straight and narrow. Gruesome but memorable was that moment when he talked of plucking out one's own evil eye or cutting off a misbehaving hand.

However, don't initially be as hard on others for any misdeeds they inflict on you, he warned. Be magnanimous, that is how they will learn quickest. Show them unlimited respect and love at all times. Gradually they will reciprocate and all the world will become a better place.

Would you believe…he then predicted yet another trap we might fall into. Feeling superior on spotting the splinter in another's eye but not recognising the beam in one's own. Self-satisfaction may

lead to hypocrisy, which is a big fault he detects in the Pharisees and Sadducees. Instead, whenever you get the chance and feel the need, put yourself back on the right path, he instructed, by going off into a quiet place to pray to the Father who knows your every requirement and will forgive your failings if you are forgiving others. 'The birds in the air, the grasses and lilies in the fields, they don't worry about tomorrow, so neither should you,' he memorably reminded us.

In summary, treat others as you would wish to be treated yourself. But don't be a soft touch. 'Build your house on rock, not sand,' he instructed. 'Develop good judgement, do the Father's will and in due time you will enter the kingdom of Heaven.'

In contrast to the usual hustle and bustle of the typical heaving crowd, this particular group listened in total respect, utter silence. His message sank deep into those lucky souls. No one there was unchanged. More than ever, I knew this new lifestyle of discipleship would be not only the most challenging but also the most rewarding time of my life.

Looking ahead, perhaps with more disciples to swell the ranks of his inner circle, I foresee even greater excitement. A nation transformed… is that too much to hope?

Andrew, a disciple of Jesus

═══════Footnote═══════

As a follower of John the Baptist, Andrew was especially happy to heed the call once John had pointed to Jesus as the 'Lamb of God'.

Most famously, he was the disciple who spotted the little boy with the five loaves and two fishes.

Supposedly, he was martyred on an X-shaped cross in Greece, whence his body was taken to Constantinople, whose patron saint he became, along with Scotland, Russia and others.

47

The first shall be last...

Goodness, I am so confused. A bit ashamed too. Not a good mix.

When I gave up my previous life to follow Jesus, I really did not appreciate just how demanding he would be. A task master like no other. 'Thaddeus, come and become one of my disciples,' he invited. 'Say 'no' to your old life...pick up your cross...a hard challenge, but you won't regret it.'

Of course, it has been exciting to go everywhere in the forefront of his band of followers, to be greeted and adulated by hundreds beset by the vagaries of life and seeking desperately for encouraging new answers to all their problems... trapped between traditional religious leaders enforcing strict Jewish customs on the one hand and harsh Roman overlordship on the other. For underdogs especially, Jesus has such a liberating message. Giving them a certainty that the least, the poor, the meek have real value beyond their lowly earthly status.

Ah yes, that word 'status'. It has been such a stumbling block to the integrity of us all. Actually, everything came to a head recently. In a nutshell, Jesus explained that little children are as important as the wisest of adults. But that has been hard to accept. Is a young shepherd boy really the equal of a Pharisee? A bit counter-intuitive. Let me think it through. Are all the struggling people we encounter, those that need healing by Jesus, really on a par with those of us who are ministering to them? And amongst his full travelling entourage, surely we twelve disciples evoke more credibility than women and others who carry out

important, yes, but ultimately menial day-to-day tasks on the group's behalf?

Worse than that, yesterday, out of Jesus' earshot, a row broke out amongst us disciples over who was the most important. Well, I have never been one of the front runners like Simon Peter or John. Some of them do seem more dedicated and worthy than I am, having also been disciples of John the baptiser previously. Nevertheless, as we argued while wandering along, I felt embarrassed by those who tried to claim special status for themselves. Our leader soon put them straight.

I find it all rather strange, because Jesus himself sets such a different example. He deliberately seeks out the most damaged, underprivileged, despised in society, then invites them in and treats them like royalty. Love your neighbour as yourself. That is his message. Hospitality personified, so much so that the powers-that-be, Jewish or Roman, are completely wrong-footed. Fair enough, though, for those in exalted positions to be irritated, maybe. But why are we, who are with Jesus day and night, observing his equanimity even in the most trying circumstances…why are we equally uncomprehending?

But for me that isn't the most puzzling thing. He now tells us that he is as one with his Father in heaven, yet must expect to die on a hated Roman cross and then be resurrected on the third day to atone for mankind's sins. Such a lot to take in. Am I up to being part of all this? His future prospect sounds horrifying, frightening. It would be the cruellest of fates…is it genuinely the plan? How could it possibly be effective? Hard to credit for a humble mortal like me, just very average till now.

So much still to learn. Though, as the months go by, I suppose I am gradually coming to terms with the full meaning of the mission behind this extraordinary healer, this teller of parables, this inspiration to individual or crowd alike, exhorting us to faithful prayer, humble repentance and selfless service. Beyond that, a suffering servant is he, as foretold by the prophets? Not at all the obvious way to confront the world in these dangerous times, but just maybe the way of the world to come…a heaven on earth, with lion and lamb at peace, one with another?

Life with Jesus has amazed me already. Must I brace myself for even more revelations in the months ahead? I sense a lot more responsibility might be coming my way.

Thaddeus, a disciple of Jesus

Footnote

Twelve key disciples held sway amongst a wider close following of both men and women, yet we hear little in the gospels about how the less prominent amongst them, like Thaddeus, may have felt over hierarchical tendencies. Nor do we hear much about their personal contributions.

Feeding crowds...

On recently coming of age, I find myself contemplating my Jewish faith more closely. Proud of those heroes of yesteryear - setting an example from boyhood onwards. David braving the giant Goliath armed with only slingshot and stones. Joseph recovering from being sold into slavery by his brothers, no less. Eli serving faithfully in the Temple from a very young age. Moses being rescued from the most precarious of starts in the Nile by a traditional enemy's own daughter. And so many others, as I have learned during my time in the synagogue school.

More than ever, I now value my home life too. Glad of my sisters' helping our mother with baking bread and weaving at the back of the house. Or entertaining the baby with a rattle, and singing soft lullabies. Whilst I stride out from the front with my father into the fields, helping to look after the communal flocks and tending the newborn lambs, calves and kids.

It's all been a happy routine. But recently I have been made aware of some extraordinary disruption building up throughout the area. All because a couple of local men, previously unremarkable, have suddenly gone on a mission! About 30, so certainly not young hotheads. The first, John, devout but much the wilder of the two, inspired thousands to follow him and to be baptised in the Jordan. Eventually including the other one, his cousin Jesus who, I gather, experienced a life-changing affirmation from God amidst that ritual there.

And now, with John arrested by the authorities - fearful of his rabble-rousing influence - then imprisoned and beheaded, this Jesus is spearheading the growing crusade. I can't help but think of him at my age not long ago, eldest to lots of brothers and sisters and helping his father - a carpenter and builder - just like I do. Though certainly more precocious than myself in the synagogue in nearby Nazareth, baffling even to his parents! But now, defying the uneasiness of the rabbis, he and his followers tour the neighbourhood villages, healing and preaching to anyone who will listen. Has it all been long planned, I wonder?

Recently, I saw him close-up. The usual crowds had been waiting by the lake...and then followed him up into the very hills where I was tending my sheep. Noisy, chaotic, a bit scary, but a chance, I felt, not to be missed. Suddenly, as Jesus stepped up onto a vantage point and raised his arms, a miraculous hush fell over us all. His address was inspirational...but more than that. Loving God means loving one another, we were told. And, as if in instant demonstration, when thoughts eventually turned to hunger, all were fed from our apparently meagre resources. One or two near him, including myself, had offered our lunchtime flatbread and fish, till in no time the food supplies were unaccountably overflowing.

I am in turmoil. The story goes that this Jesus was visited by shepherds like me at his birth in a stable-cave in Bethlehem. I feel a bond there! He is maybe not the Messiah the zealots were expecting but he seems to be transcending all that. Both following yet relaxing the strictest rules we Jews have long observed. Setting an example more fundamental and universal. The whole world needs to hear him, I reckon. Maybe will!

A Galilean shepherd

Footnote

Though famed for often teaching in the synagogue himself, Jesus clearly raised opposition amongst other religious leaders.

His earthly mission arose in a small geographical area, where he had been known personally to many in normal daily life for years before his more radical ministry began. Thus there is a striking ambivalence in the willingness of people to honour (or not) a 'prophet in his own land'.

BROTHER, SISTER,
LET ME SERVE YOU...

Caught in the Act...

I have only myself to blame for nearly losing my life today. I was seconds away from being killed in blood and pain and terror.

Impetuous, careless, reckless I had been, I know. All due to my weakness in not being able to give up my existing lover completely as soon as my father had arranged for me to marry a rich stranger I hardly knew. Instead, one secret assignation had led to another and another. Until inevitably I was caught in the very act. My lover was lucky, for now at least, because he managed to run way. In fact, he stood to face the same penalty as me, under our strict laws.

Anyway, the priests lost no time in deciding to use me as a new pawn in their determination to trip up the amazingly popular new preacher… with increasing desperation, they bitterly resented, no hated, his threat to their authority. Still do. They dragged me to the Temple precincts and flung me down in front of this Jesus and the growing crowd that had been gathering round to listen to his teaching. The very sort of folk in whose eyes they particularly wanted to discredit him. 'The law of Moses says to stone her. What do you say?' they demanded. But fortunately for me, showing no sign of the pressure, he proceeded to pass judgement in a most unexpected way.

How come? Why was that? Well, forgiveness is one of his key messages but in tackling my situation it was against a tricky back-story. The cynics say he probably carries a guilty conscience over the rumours that his own mother-to-be had once misbehaved scandalously too. Mysteriously pregnant before her marriage. She had been very lucky, many feel. Because, despite having been cuckolded, the man to whom she was betrothed forgave her, kept everything secret, and then engineered her escape from any lingering risk of rough justice by whisking them both off to Egypt straight after the baby was born. So, thirty years later, the preacher's many critics among the priests are appalled but not wholly surprised in hindsight that he behaved towards me so leniently, in their opinion. But in the present moment, there seemed no prospect that my life would not be forfeit. In truth, against all the odds, Jesus simply outwitted the angry accusers.

Of course, this morning I was terrified. The Pharisees were sensing triumph. The crowd was simmering. On the edge. A few were already looking round for stones. Only Jesus remained calm. Biding his time, he stooped down and wrote something in the dust. Was there any chance he might prevent disaster, I wondered? I cowered helplessly as people started to shuffle forwards. Tension all around. In mounting despair, I glanced up. And saw the compassion on Jesus's face, the empathy in his eyes. Was there still hope for me? There seemed precious little prospect as an ugly mood continued to build.

'Stop stalling!' the Pharisees demanded. 'What is your answer?' Only to be thrown into confusion by his challenge to the whole crowd. 'All right, let the one who has never sinned cast the first stone.' Stunned silence…while Jesus stayed cool, stooped down and wrote in the dust again. At first, no one moved. He had rendered them all inactive by those few words. Slowly, the oldest, then one or two more, then a growing trickle slipped away. Bizarrely, under the circumstances, in much pensive shame themselves. Even the Pharisees.

Finally, I found myself alone with Jesus. Incredulous. I was in floods of tears. Partly the release of so much emotional tension, partly in

gratitude. With no trace of triumph, he quietly said, 'Where are your accusers? Didn't even one of them condemn you?' Hardly able to believe it, I stuttered in reply, 'No, Lord.' And he said, 'Then neither do I. Go now and sin no more.'

A chance for me to reassess my priorities. To resist that obsession with my lover. My husband is not a bad man. He provides well for me. I am ashamed that it took a glimpse of death's door to realise that. I won't betray him again.

After all, it would mean letting Jesus down too.

Woman caught in adultery

Footnote

The ultimate teaching to avoid self-righteousness and hypocrisy. And an example of God's reconciliation through Jesus.

Analysing textual style, some scholars say this story is an add-on to John's gospel 100 years later.

Uɲɢlean...

Only now I am cured can I bear to think back to that disastrous day years ago when the priest declared me unclean. I had initially approached him in dread. Leprosy was my fear. I knew it was a terrible and defiling disease. If I were judged infected, I would be both physically and ceremonially ostracised. Was it God's punishment for my sins? To my utter despair, the priest's final damning verdict duly condemned me to a living death. In fact, curing a leper was regarded as so unlikely that it equated to raising a person from the dead.

So, for years I was excluded from normal society, living in a cave, begging, often ringing my bell to warn clean people not to approach me whenever I ventured out. My shabby appearance spoke volumes anyway. My tattered clothes. My half-face mask. My matted hair. My shambling gait too. No need for anyone to see the patchy, pussy skin on my face to know to avoid me. There was no arrangement or commandment to take care of me and my kind. We tended to form our own communities, begging for food, somehow surviving, but nothing more.

Then, one day recently on a nearby hillside I saw a commotion around a travelling preacher who seemed to be looking favourably on and healing some hitherto hopeless cases, to judge by the amazed cries of the crowds. Perhaps he wouldn't be like the Pharisees, obsessed with the strict purity laws. Perhaps the needs of people mattered more to him than the letter of the Law. Was he someone who could be my one and only chance, my salvation? I convinced myself of it.

But there was no way I could ask anyone about him. No way I could mingle with the crowds. No way I could get a message to him. It seemed hopeless. Unless, unless… Yes, I would have to waylay him when he was walking along with just his immediate circle. So one day I did just that, to the horror of his disciples who tried desperately to usher me away. But the healer showed none of their revulsion.

I would normally shout 'Unclean, unclean', if approaching anyone. But on that occasion I felt inspired with a totally unprecedented confidence. 'Make me clean,' I demanded of him. 'If you are willing.' What happened next was beyond my wildest hopes. He came up close and stretched out his hand towards me. Then, as I knelt, he actually touched me! He broke that taboo, just for a pathetic-looking creature like me. I suppose he felt my overwhelming faith in him, in his ability to heal me. 'I am willing,' he said. 'Be cleansed.' And it happened. I felt his power flow through me, replacing all that impurity. I like to think we achieved the transformation between us. It was a miracle.

His followers were staggered by the risk they felt he was taking for someone so unworthy, but he used my situation to teach them an important lesson. No one is too inferior, no one is too far gone, no one is too unloved. His mercy, his saving grace is universal. And to their everlasting credit, when they saw Jesus embracing me in joy and tenderness, they hugged me too.

'Tell nobody,' he instructed me. 'Just go back to the priest. The first two purification rites are effectively done. Just the third phase to go. Take him a sacrifice. And he will anoint you with blood and oil. Then you are free to join any community again.'

I am back from the dead.

A grateful leper

Footnote

The concept of purity has been transposed from a cultic to an ethical level.

In the Sermon on the Mount, Jesus said, 'Blessed are the pure in heart, for they will see God.' A teaching that absorbs, then transcends the Law with its emphasis on external ceremonial cleaning.

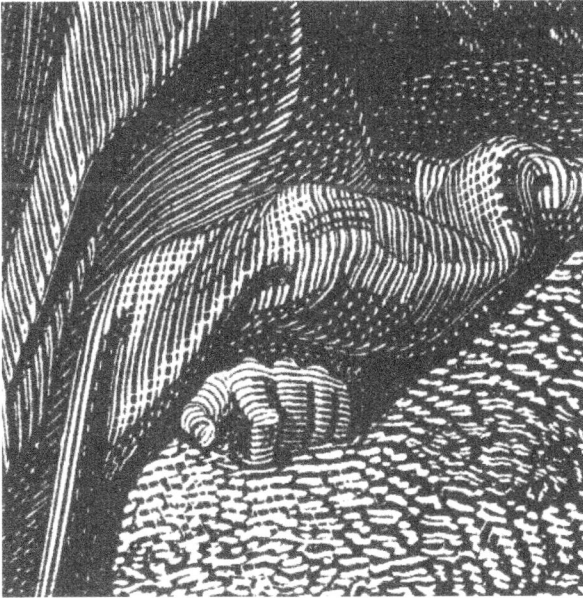

Dead or alive...

I could never repay the man. I thank the Lord that Jesus's reputation had gone ahead of him. It was as he disembarked after one of his frequent trips across the Sea of Galilee that the whisper of his arrival reached me…at such an opportune moment. I dashed down to the shore and put myself at his mercy. I needed his help…fast.

Some of us who have responsible roles in the synagogue are perhaps understandably suspicious of his motives and unorthodox behaviour, and I was initially one such. But that day I was so desperate as I sought nothing less than a miracle. Who better? I told myself. Falling at his feet, I pleaded, 'My daughter is about to die. Please, please lay your hands on her, rescue her and let her live.' And he agreed to come with me, back to my house, to her sickbed. My hopes rose.

She had always been a perfectly healthy girl till recently. But, at the age of twelve, she had just been showing the first physical signs of womanhood and that was all going drastically wrong. Her blood loss was so excessive that it had made her incredibly weak. In next to no time, in front of our despairing gaze, she looked to be knocking on death's door. All the ideas for a potential remedy had been exhausted. We were just waiting for the worst.

Of course, that day as usual, wherever he set off for, a huge crowd continued to follow, pushing and shoving to get closer to him. Then, extraordinarily, one woman's slight touch on his clothes caused him to

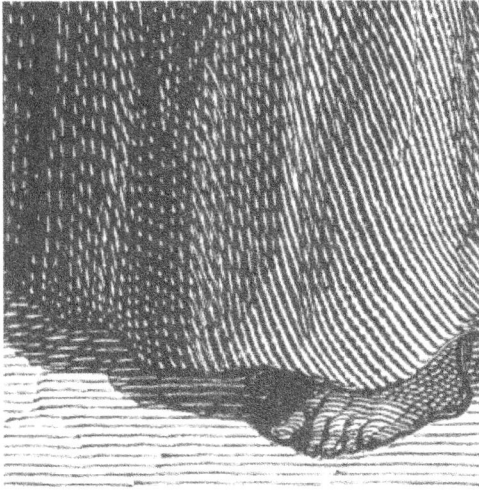

stop instantly. To my shame, I resented her. But Jesus insisted on hearing her story. Afraid and trembling, she explained how much she had suffered. Apparently, from twelve years of non-stop bleeding…equivalent to my daughter's whole lifetime. A very brave confession. I'm sure she had been terrified that he would be unwilling to associate himself with someone so ritually unclean. She need not have worried. He always took a more holistic approach to people's problems. Managing to hold back her fears of immediate rejection, she had grasped her golden opportunity, feeling sure that just to touch his garments would be enough for a cure. And it was. 'Your faith has rescued you. Go in peace. Be healed,' he reassured her. And, though I abhorred the delay to our progress, my own confidence and faith soared. It seemed a premonition. Was the solution indeed at his fingertips? Then suddenly, disaster. A messenger from my house rushed up to say that my daughter had just died. It was all too late. Forgive my human weakness in fleetingly blaming the woman who had caused that extra delay.

Amazingly, however, Jesus was not dismayed. 'Jairus, don't be afraid. Just believe.' So, with the most trusted three of his disciples, we pressed on. Only at the door to behold everyone wailing and weeping. Including professional mourners with their flutes. It all seemed very final. They jeered when he claimed, 'She is only sleeping.' Nevertheless, our little group went inside to join my wife at the bedside. Where he simply took the child's hand and quietly said, 'Kalitha toum…Time to get up, little

girl.' And the grief I had been holding back flowed in a torrent of tears as she got up, walked about and asked for something to eat. Minutes before, all was lost. Now, against the odds, we anticipated soon being able to rejoice with our friends and relatives.

My stunned household circle was astonished. However, recovering quickly, it seemed natural for us to be rushing out to tell the world… till Jesus commanded that we must keep our excitement in check. 'Stay low key. Don't make any special efforts to spread the news.' The request seemed counter-intuitive, but how could I refuse him anything after what he had done to save not only my daughter's life but also my whole family's sanity?

Jairus, a synagogue leader

═Footnote═

Clearly Jesus realises that his enemies, including Herod, would feel threatened by his increasing influence in the area. Would his progress around even be blocked by force?

This miracle is an example of Jesus being prepared to take action encompassing a wider view of someone's need, rather than be bound by a strict interpretation of Jewish laws.

The account makes us ponder on his own encounter with death, cheating it in a unique way with such everlasting consequences.

Down among the demons...

Haunting the graveyard amongst all those departed souls. Tragically, it felt like the right habitat for a damned nutcase like me. Sometimes I ventured onto the hillside and everyone there scattered in terror. Hour after hour I screamed and shouted at a bloodcurdling volume. A few brave folk had tried to shackle me, but with my superhuman strength I swiftly snapped even the strongest of chains. In the depths of self loathing, I slashed myself with stones. A gory, bloody, scruffy, shambolic, rowdy nuisance to the whole neighbourhood. The personification of unclean. Possessed by so many demons, I was known as Legion. Surely I was locked for ever into a life that was simply not worth living.

Then one day, quite unexpectedly, I sensed hope. Someone approaching from a distance at the head of a small group was confronting my demons, commanding them to leave me alone at once. Actually, it was throwing me into even more turmoil than usual. Enraged, I ran madly towards him and, do you know, all his followers backed off but he never so much as blinked. 'Come out of him!' he kept demanding.

Now, coincidentally on the hillside was a large herd of pigs. Not a rare sight in the Decapolis but the epitome of uncleanliness to a Jew, which I suspected him to be. And before I could fully grasp his intentions, my demons transferred into them. A wild dash of two thousand pigs streamed past, gathering pace down the steep slope. Unable to stop, they all swept into the Sea of Galilee and were drowned. It took a while for anyone to comprehend what they had witnessed. Not least me. Except perhaps the herdsmen whose immediate livelihood it all threatened. Baffled and distraught, they fled off into town to tell the tale. And recount the effects of the mayhem. Whip up a protest.

From all around people soon came flocking to the spot. To share in the inevitable commotion that now ensued. To witness the bodies of the dead pigs in the water. To marvel at the sight of me, stunned but certainly at that moment the most sober man amongst them.

In fact, they were also afraid. 'Go home, Jew,' they said to my saviour. Now their aggression was frightening me. 'Please can I come with you?' I pleaded with the man. But he refused. Wouldn't let me be dependent on him for a moment longer. Told me to go home and show people in the surrounding towns the dramatic transformation that had occurred in me. My life turned round by the mercy he had lavished on my desperate situation. Demonstrate to everyone I met the healing miracle that had taken place. How he had saved me from my madness. Be an ongoing witness beyond his homeland. No one would be less than totally astonished.

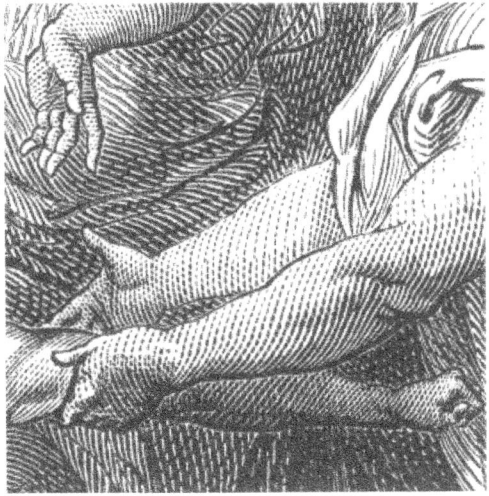

And as I stood transfixed but resolutely determined to carry out his wishes, he bade me farewell, quietly turned around and led his men away from the hustle and bustle. Minutes later, they boarded their boats and sailed back to their own country. Lesson taught, lesson learned.

Legion, a demoniac

══════Footnote══════

The east side of the Sea of Galilee was not Jewish land. So this story is a small symbol of the healing power that Christ's message can bring to everyone's situation.

How ironic that at the end of his own earthly life, Jesus himself would be in tortured agony of body and mind, his flesh bleeding and his sanity threatened. Receiving a devastating persecution on behalf of all generations.

Up a fig tree...

I am very proud of my birthplace, Jericho. Highly favoured by God in being granted to our ancestors as the first city conquered after crossing the Jordan river and occupying the Promised Land. Attractive today as a fertile, spring fed oasis near Jerusalem, with an abundance of palm trees. Business-wise, it is brilliantly sited at a strategic crossroads location, controlling important migration routes. Additionally, the lucrative production and export of balsam is centred here.

I didn't have any contacts in high places but I felt sure that I could carve out a lucrative career in the town if I made a few compromises. Chiefly, confronting that big dilemma...the resented Romans being in control. But 'Render unto Caesar that which is Caesar's' seems to be a mantra doing the rounds. So, I soon realised and accepted that to get rich my best bet would be to work for them, collecting taxes. I knew they wouldn't pay me an actual wage. Nevertheless, the system was open to exploitation by someone as shrewd as myself. On top of their dues, I could demand extra money and keep most of it for myself. Bit of dishonesty, bit of abuse never went amiss. Gradually I worked my way up the ladder until eventually I became a chief tax collector. You should see the house I bought with all my accumulated wealth!

The downside is obvious. My fellow Jews inevitably despised me. Partly for helping the hated foreign regime, partly for my unscrupulousness. And over the years it has all preyed increasingly on my conscience, but what to do about it?

Then, recently I heard that the famous itinerant preacher, Jesus, was due to pass through town on his way to Jerusalem. Somehow I began to feel he may be able to help my quandary. Naturally, most of the local populace was curious to see and hear him too and I knew a big crowd was likely to gather round. It wouldn't be easy to meet him...none of his followers were going to be willing to help someone as unpopular as me. Not only that, I am not of the tallest. I might not even manage a glimpse. My only hope would be to get in position as early as possible and climb a convenient roadside sycamore fig tree to get a decent view. It worked even better than I could have hoped. He spied me, addressed me by name, 'Zacchaeus,' and called me down. How notorious must I be, I silently wondered. And how brave of him to associate with me. Then, beyond my wildest expectations, he invited himself to my house! How could he be prepared to sully himself by being the guest of a sinner? An even more remarkable man than I had been expecting, I thought to myself.

No way, though, was I going to let the chance to talk with him pass me by. In private conversation eventually he told me one of his parables. A Pharisee and a tax collector went to the temple to pray. The former prayed about how virtuous he was., observing the law, fasting twice a week and giving tithes. 'I am not like other men - robbers, evil-doers and adulterers.' But the tax collector put his head down in a gesture of contrition, asking for God's mercy on a sinner. On that basis, with that repentance, Jesus said that it was the tax collector who would go home justified by God. 'Everyone who exalts himself will be humbled, and he who humbles himself will be exalted.'

That was the turning point for me. He has transformed my life. Cleansed my soul, you might say. From now on, no more cheating. Honesty in everything. And I will make an immediate start on helping those less fortunate than myself by giving away half my wealth. In due course, maybe more.

Zacchaeus, a tax collector

Footnote

At the original Jericho site today there is a large, venerable square tower, which by tradition is named the House of Zacchaeus.

And in Eastern Christianity his gospel story is read on or around the last Sunday preceding the liturgical preparation for Lent...the first stage of a new Paschal cycle.

Sometimes in Western Christianity the reading is used at the dedication of a Church or on its anniversary.

In Southern Bavaria there is even a special flag of red with a white cross.

Perhaps with a certain irony, the name means 'pure'.

Water at the well...

After a volatile life with five very demanding husbands and now a live-in partner, I am unsurprisingly rather cynical and wary about menfolk. But in a recent quite unexpected encounter, I found myself irresistibly impressed by an enigmatic Jew.

We met by chance in the mid-day sun at Jacob's well, where I had gone to draw water. He was alone because his followers had left him behind to rest while they went into town for food. And immediately he asked my name, Photine, then flouted every custom by asking me, a mere Samaritan woman, for a simple drink.

I realise it was the hottest part of the day, but I now know he was really using the ploy to teach me a spiritual lesson. I had already sensed he might be a prophet but his claims went far beyond even what that role entails. He started to describe a mysterious sort of living water that bestowed not just thirst quenching satisfaction but everlasting life. Incredible. From God, his Father, he continued. Naturally I asked for some, but he explained it was all bound up so far with the way that only the Jews worshipped in spirit and truth and thereby received salvation. And he dismissed my quibble that worship could take place just as effectively here on the mountain as in their city of Jerusalem.

At first it all seemed rather excluding. But suddenly the pieces fitted together. Into my mind flashed a rumour I had heard that a Messiah would one day come to proclaim such revelations. Why was I not surprised when he went on to say, 'I am he, the one who is speaking to you'?

At my time of life it is amazing to me that all my prejudices against men have been swept away by this encounter. When his followers returned to the well, I joined them, aspiring eventually to be their equal. Impossible not to want to leave my past experiences behind and be a small part of this Jesus's crusade. To strive to bring many others to a life-saving, life-giving, life-enhancing faith in him. Offering the living water to everyone so that no one need ever be thirsty again.

Photine, a Samaritan woman

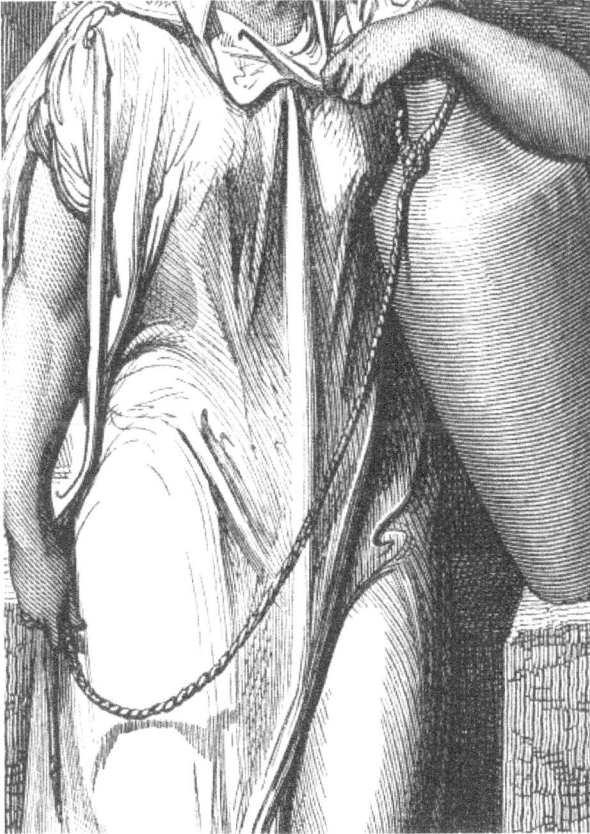

Footnote

In Eastern Orthodox and Eastern Catholic traditions, Photine, meaning 'luminous', is venerated as a saint, despite her less than wholesome early lifestyle.

But of course her encounter with Jesus transformed her into a devoted follower. 'Come and see a man who has told me everything I have ever done...' she says in the aftermath of that cleansing experience with the living water of grace.

Tradition also holds that she was finally brought before Emperor Nero to answer for her faith and was tortured, then with bitter irony died a martyr after being thrown down a dry well.

Pool...

As a very proud Jew, I am excited by the possibilities in following a new leader, Jesus, because I can instinctively sense that he is a zealous type like myself. Within the Law, but a pragmatic free thinker too. Whatever difficulties threaten, whatever opposition looms, I know he will remain on course. Not be cowed by the overbearing Romans. But what surprises me is the way he combines that with compassion at all times. And recently I was humbled to witness his healing powers at first hand when Jesus had travelled to Jerusalem for a festival.

I have an older brother, Jesse, who has been dogged by illness all his life. So much so that he eventually became almost paralysed and spent most of his waking life at the Pool of Bethesda, just north of the Temple Mount, in the shade of its five covered colonnades. A desperately sad sight to see so many blind and lame and sick, scattered around the sacred springs with their shallow pools and baths. Praying or chanting to the spirits in the hope of a cure. And, being festival time, it was especially busy with large crowds refreshing and ritually cleansing themselves.

That day I found Jesus and took my anguished fears to him. Told him how helpless I felt. How I could no longer bear to visit my brother there. To watch him lying on his mat, trying to anticipate that special moment when the spring would suddenly bubble up and agitate the surface of a pool. All the time knowing he would never be quick enough to race all the other invalids down the steps into the water in their mad hope that the first to reach that particular spot would be cured. Soul destroying to witness such utter hopelessness. Nearly thirty eight years Jesse had suffered. Nothing was likely to change now.

Jesus listened to my grief. That was very calming in itself. But he wasn't leaving it there. 'Let's go to the pool,' he quietly encouraged. 'Give Jesse our support. See how he is today.' Somehow I sensed a turning point, just feeling his authority being brought to bear on the situation. And when we got there, his presence and positivity made me start to tingle all over. It would happen. Jesse would feel it too, I just knew. I held myself back to observe. They had never met before. But, joy to behold…as all the other anguished folk and the healthy visitors alike watched in amazement, Jesus walked slowly over to him. Simply posed the salient challenge, 'After so long, do you really want to be well?' Then, allowing no time for denial or hesitation, he instructed, 'Take up your bed and walk.' I couldn't comprehend what I next witnessed. Probably no one else could believe their eyes either. Because instantly Jesse defied the lifetime of inactivity, pain, feebleness. Picked up his mat and calmly walked away. Trust, faith! I followed, speechless. Elation soon took over, just a few minutes later. Jesus meanwhile had slipped away, avoiding any fuss.

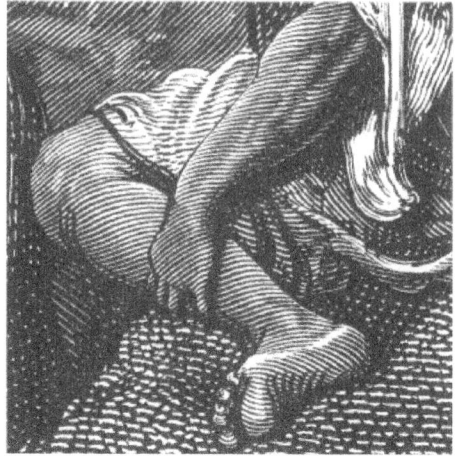

I can't credit the unfortunate ensuing complication though. A couple of priests stopped Jesse and told him he shouldn't be carrying his mat on the Sabbath. 'Who encouraged you to break the Law?' they demanded. Luckily, Jesse didn't know. But later Jesus met him at the Temple and gave him some spiritual advice to complete the cure. I'm embarrassed to confess that Jesse then went straight to the priests to satisfy their previously unanswered question. Partly out of a sense of obligation, I suppose, but maybe, more charitably, as I hope, to praise his name in further belated thanks.

Sadly, Jesus's free thinking action, above all to do good, as I fully realise, had served only to enrage them. They began to plot more ways to persecute him. With implications too for all his disciples and followers, no doubt. But then he never promised that following him would be easy.

Simon the Zealot, a disciple of Jesus

Footnote

Not to be confused with Simon Peter or one of Jesus's brothers, little is recorded about Simon the Zealot. Though there was certainly a strong undercurrent, the nationalistic movement implied in his name probably didn't exist formally in Jesus's day.

His missionary work perhaps took place mainly in Egypt.

Possible martyrdom fates are rumoured for Iberia, Persia, Samaria, even Britain, though Eastern custom claims he died of old age in Edessa.

In art he is associated with a saw, following the tradition of his martyrdom through being sawn in half.

Talking Point

A healing ministry...

Judaism has a long history of prayers and rituals for healing, based on the connection between the body and the soul. A holistic message, focusing on compassion and community sharing. Illness brings multiple losses, not just physical but also social, and healing involves a divine encounter. Jesus was in that sacred tradition - an archetypal Jew bringing meaning to life in the face of suffering, along with an understanding of how God relates to humanity. But in a fresh way - new wine in old skins.

Jesus's miracles defy the laws of even today's medical theories and practices. He adds the power of belief and trust (in its more mundane way, the placebo effect also relies on that). He confirms to the woman with blood issues that her faith has cured her. Similarly, the military official (unlike the agitated lute-players) helps raise his 'dead' daughter by his clear expectation. And the blind and deaf men are transformed through trust too. No inhibition, incidentally, for Jesus in dealing with, to conventional Jews, unclean people and situations.

Sad, as he went round healing, that Jesus found everyone dejected, without leadership or a shepherd. But he brought optimism to that poor Galilean area of a downtrodden country under the Roman yoke. In his day he didn't manage to free his people or establish a kingdom of heaven on earth as many were anticipating, but he did inspire them with a healing hope. And what a fascinating example to set, in that he actually conscripted a tax-collector, a despised figure on the side of the enemy.

Jesus travelled the area, followed by ever larger crowds, but as yet insufficient - plenty of harvest but not many workers...praying for more to harvest his fields. And the miracles were an expected but very powerful tool in that quest...the crowds were amazed etc. So, one obvious question arises. Why did he issue a stern warning at one point to take care that nobody gets to know about this? It was ignored, but was he really afraid that his miracles were being credibly credited to the prince of demons? Interestingly, in ch10 v1 of Matthew we learn that in future the disciples too will be casting out unclean spirits and healing every sickness. No doubt in that classic Jewish mould.

A closing lesson, appropriate to our current world situation. Think holistic. Remain upbeat. Express hope. Keep the faith. Support one another. Disease can be cured. Solutions can be found. Set an example of positivity, whether over pandemics or climate change or conflict.

LORD, TEACH US...

Parables in brief...

Hidden Treasures

A man once got lucky and found
Buried treasure deep down in the ground.
So that made him quite glad
To sell all that he had
And to purchase the fields all around.

Matthew 13 v 44

Labourers in the Vineyard

A silver coin payment to all,
No matter at what hour I call,
'Cause whenever you came,
My fair wage is the same
And the vineyard's for great and for small.

Matthew 20 v 1-16

Parable of the Net

An angel once threw out his net
To test just what fish he might get,
And the bad of the catch
He made plans to despatch
To a bucket or fire they'd regret.

Matthew 13 v 47-50

Pearls before Swine

It's sad that dogs put to the test
Turn and bite when they're offered the best,
And the same with pigs when,
Given pearls in their pen,
They just trample them down where they've messed.

Matthew 7 v 6

Fed and Nurtured

Whatever anxious thoughts you think
Because you have few coins to chink…
As I care for all flow'rs,
And the birds at all hours,
I promise you clothes, food and drink.

Matthew 6 v 25-32

Sheep and Goats

As the shepherd weeds goats from the sheep,
So the Lord rejects bad, good to keep,
'Cause when He was right there
With a need for some care,
They were blind; so now...fiery deep.

Matthew 25 v 31-46

Ten Young Women

The bridegroom came late in the night,
Only five still had oil for their light.
The rest hadn't a drop
Till they'd been to the shop.
When they got back, the door was shut tight.

Matthew 25 v 1-13

Treasures Old and New

Don't jump straight to judgement too fast,
With only laws not fit to last.
In this new house of mine,
With fresh skins for the wine,
The present comes forth with the past.

Matthew 13 v 52

Two Sons

Thanks, Jesus, but don't think I will;
Obey you, that is, not until...
Ah, I've now changed my mind.
That's much better, I find,
Than to say Yes, and then to stand still.

Matthew 21 v 28-31

Wheat and Tares

When the enemy mixes the seed,
The wheat will grow next to the weed,
But the harvesters choose
Which bad plants they must lose...
Using God's crop, the hungry to feed.

Matthew 13 v 24-30

Talents

Talents two up to four, five to ten.
The Master was pleased with those men.
But the man who had one
Hid it, nothing got done.
He was banished, seen never again.

Matthew 25 v 14-30

Solid Foundations

The rain fell, the floods came, the winds blew
On house built to stay firm and true,
Set on rock, not on sand,
Every storm to withstand.
So, in Jesus you'll know what to do.

Matthew 7 v 24-29

Unlikely Rescuer

The Jericho road can be rough.
Some assailants took all a Jew's stuff.
Priest and Levite walked on,
Help in need came there none.
But Samaritan…more than enough.

Luke 10 v 29-37

Prodigal Son

Inheritance wasted, my boy?
Your lifestyle of old thus destroy?
But I'm here you to greet,
Fatted calf killed to eat.
Lost, now found…take fresh gifts and enjoy.

Luke 15 v 11-32

God and Money

Use your money to earn people's trust,
So they help you, if ever you're bust.
But such wealth's not the best
When you're put to the test.
Serving God as your Master's the must

Luke 16 v 9-13

The Lamp

As the town on the hill shines out bright,
So the lamp on its stand you must light.
To illuminate all
On your house who may call.
Thus to glorify God day and night.

Mark 4 v 21-25

The Sower

The seed on the path feeds a bird.
On the rock is no better, I've heard.
With no soil it can't grow,
Midst the thorns is a no,
In the good ground is greatly preferred.

Mark 4 v 1-20

Dives

The poor man on earth he had spurned,
So the rich man in Hades lay burned.
Warn my brothers in haste,
Lest they fall to this place!
No, through prophets such lessons are learned.

Luke 12 v 13-21

Fig Tree

Like the fig tree on long planted roots
That stubbornly bore too few fruits,
God allows one last try,
To succeed bye and bye,
Or He'll no longer work in cahoots.

Mark 13 v 28-31

Fruitfulness

Just as Cana's guests savoured best wine,
Changed from water through actions of mine.
So ought those in pursuit,
Who would bear the best fruit,
Be strong branches attached to my vine.

John 2 v 1-10. John 15 v 1-8

The Lost Sheep

Hundred sheep owe their care to their boy,
Safe from enemies out to destroy,
'Cause he worries on days
An unwary one strays.
Found...he carries it home to great joy.

Luke 15 v 4-7

Coins

To offer your all is quite right,
Like the widow who gave her last mite.
As for those that abhor
That lost coin on the floor,
They must search for it, rolled out of sight.

Luke 21 v 1-4, Luke 15 v 8-10

Pounds

Ten pounds I entrust to each one
To invest for me while I am gone.
Two did well and made more.
The last put it in store,
So was damned and was left holding none.

Luke 19 v 11-27

OFT IN DANGER,
OFT IN WOE...

Three siblings...

Jerusalem is such a busy place, and not only at Passover time. So my sisters Martha and Mary and I have always appreciated the convenience of living in nearby Bethany. It offers a peaceful everyday lifestyle along with those city benefits a short distance away, as well as being on the road to Jericho. In fact, we are much in demand as a stopover for many visiting friends.

Of course, I shall be eternally grateful to one in particular. My life-saver in every sense. Though I rely for the details on what my sisters have told me subsequently, I still feel traumatised to recall the circumstances even now. I break out in a cold sweat whenever anyone starts to mention its unique denouement. Some even call it a resurrection event...

A little while ago I was taken ill with a severely debilitating sickness. So extreme was it that I lay immobile in bed for several weeks, increasingly feverish and hopelessly enfeebled. Eventually, I am told, I fell into a coma - becoming chillingly cold to the touch. My sisters cared for me slavishly, as you would expect, but they were feeling desperate. However, fortunately for me, Mary had grown especially close to one special friend who had become an itinerant teacher with amazing healing powers. Martha too was hugely impressed by him, to such an extent that she was even sensing he could be the Messiah, the Son of God. Nothing therefore felt more natural to them in their anxiety than to send word to him about my plight, but this Jesus was days away, probably too far to intervene in time.

Meanwhile, many other friends had come flocking to support my grieving sisters, and possibly be involved in mourning for me if the worst transpired. My lifeless body had been placed in a cave, sealed by a large stone, but there was still no sign of Jesus arriving to help. Four days too late, so opinion went. Finally, rumour reached my sisters that he was approaching. Ever resourceful, Martha dashed to meet him, full of hope and trust, despite the odds. But, emotionally conflicted, she began, 'Lord, if you had been here, he wouldn't have died,' understandably unable to completely conceal her pent-up anger and frustration at the delay. 'But even now I truly believe God will give you whatever you ask.' He was equal to the challenge. 'Lazarus will rise again. Not just at the last day, but here and now. No hurry still, though. Send your beloved sister Mary to see me here.'

And Mary, balancing her similar anger and frustration with a burgeoning hope, rushed to comply. Followed by many of the would-be mourners. Surrounded by such mounting angst over my fate, Jesus was deeply moved...and wept! To this day I am so flattered to think that someone so special should feel like that about me.

The gathering crowd slowly returned to the village and went to my tomb. 'Roll away the stone,' Jesus instructed. 'But surely, after all this time the body will smell!' protested my ever practical sister. Back came the stern response, 'Did I not tell you that if you believe you will see the glory of God?' And we all heard his quiet prayer of thanks, 'Father, you have listened to me so that these people can believe that you sent me.'

'Lazarus, come out!' came the loud command. And to the amazement of everyone, there slowly appeared the weird grave-clothes covered figure of the supposedly dead man. Me! Hands and feet in linen strips, with a cloth around my face. As you might expect, I remember nothing of those comatose weeks on the threshold between life and death, but I have made a fully recovered transition to my erstwhile earthly routines. I owe so much to those very dear sisters who kept faith in me and in that divine healer.

Inevitably, the miraculous story spread like wildfire around the neighbourhood. Much more remarkably, Caiaphas, the high priest, prophesied that Jesus himself would one day die for and unite the Jewish nation. Thus a threat, in their eyes, that might alarm the Romans. To such an extent that the priests plotted to kill him. In the immediate aftermath of my being saved from death, he had to take his disciples into hiding.

No way would Jesus be intimidated for long, though. Soon he and his followers were out and about in their inimitable way. But opponents under threat often grow in their determination. I sensed from then on that a collision course had been set.

Actually, Passover is imminent again and so I have invited Jesus to stay with us for a few days beforehand. Mary is particularly concerned about his future, however, and I have noticed her preparing a special surprise for him...much to Martha's displeasure, unfortunately, as she fears it will be inappropriately extravagant. We will see how that unfolds. It could yield a spectacular story!

Beyond that, I gather he has plans to mark Passover time as another crucial stage in his God-given ministry to us all. He has asked us to source a donkey he can borrow for a symbolic dramatic entry at the start, with palm leaves strewn in front of him by cheering supporters. With provocation like that, I am definitely anticipating a major confrontation. A week like no other.

Lazarus, a friend of Jesus

Footnote

The tomb of Lazarus is a traditional pilgrimage site on the south east slopes of the Mount of Olives.

He is reputed to have spent the last 30 years of his life in Cyprus.

Epstein's sculpture of Lazarus is in New College, Oxford.

The Law...

We Pharisees must re-double our efforts. Clearly the country is in a mess because of not following the Torah strictly enough. A simple example… everyone should be fasting far more often as we await the establishment of God's kingdom. Praying harder for his mercy. Abiding by God's laws more thoroughly, without exception. In exchange for utter obedience, God will respond, the tide will turn. We tell people that message over and over again, but they find it very hard. I know nothing has borne much fruit recently. Life is obviously tough under the ruthless Roman yoke but everyone must try harder, stick together. It is particularly vital that the people obey us as their religious leaders - after all, we have spent years in studying and training…the Sadducees too. Priests know exactly what is required in the Temple. We Pharisees are distinguished by our learning and piety, exercised for the people's benefit. And everything we say or do is based on hundreds of years of Jewish tradition.

However, there is a disruptive element growing subversively in our midst. A message teaching lower standards is spreading like wildfire. If we don't manage to check it, soon it will infect our whole way of life. Make bad matters worse. The architect of all this opposition to our instructions is based in Galilee, though he does travel quite widely. We have been tailing him for a while, and it's all getting quite alarming. He is well educated, so we must take him seriously, but he pays us leaders no respect. We weren't sure whether to stop him from teaching in the synagogues, but achieved only limited success, and it's too late to concentrate on that now. As he roams around with his hard-core followers, crowds everywhere gather to listen to his boastful claims, seduced by some measure of healing sorcery.

This Jesus even disrespects the Sabbath. Thinks he is now in charge of that sacred day. He lets his disciples pick and eat ears of corn then, quoting some spurious David precedent. Last week he even healed a man with a withered hand in the middle of a synagogue... quite inappropriate behaviour. And many witnessed another scandalous episode at the Pool of Bethesda.

Recently, I invited a group of fellow Pharisees and teachers of the Law from Galilee, Judaea and elsewhere to meet at a village house where he was anticipated. Many of them hadn't realised yet how dangerous he could be, or how popular. Word had certainly got round generally, because the crowd there was huge. Completely surrounded the house that he was using as a base. So much so that one group who had come on a special mission began to get very frustrated. They were carrying a paralysed friend on a bed but couldn't push their way through. Somehow they got up onto the roof and lowered the stretcher down through it. Of course, that got this Jesus's attention. We strained to hear what he might say. Incredible. 'My friend, your sins are forgiven you.' Just words really, but unbelievable. Pure blasphemy. Only God can forgive sins. So we had to challenge him. Immediately he claimed divine authority all the more. And, to prove it, said he would convince us by curing the man. Told him, 'I order you to get up, and pick up

your stretcher and go home.' Quite a performance. I reckon he rigged it somehow. But we teachers were helpless to criticise further on the day. Not only did the man straightaway walk off glorifying God, but also the whole crowd went wild with excitement and acclamation. And sadly, totally convinced of this Jesus's claims. 'You are the Son of Man,' they shouted to him. Bit of a hero. We leaders didn't stay around to witness what other chicanery he might get up to next.

What can we do to stop him? In the face of all the euphoria he evokes in those ignorant folk, it will be quite difficult. Unfortunately, in effect he is protected by them for the time being. If anything happened to him for now, we would have a riot on our hands because suspicion would obviously fall on us. But it is our duty to restore order and total obedience to the Law. No more of that nonsense about having come to fulfil it on the one hand, yet then tweak and twist it to suit himself on the other. We need a bespoke plan. Capture him cleverly, in circumstances where our accusations will stick. A bit more patience till the right opportunity arises. It will.

A strict Pharisee

Footnote

The main sects of Judaism were the Pharisees, a lay elite concerned with a precise interpretation of the written and oral law who accepted resurrection...and the Sadducees, a more social elite drawn from the wealthy and priestly elite, who rejected the oral law and resurrection.

A third group, the Zealots, consisted of the more inflexible combative conservatives.

A fourth group, the Essenes, were more retiring and contemplative but don't feature in the New Testament. Probably lived at Qumran and compiled, then concealed, the Dead Sea scrolls.

The Servant King...

For the last twenty-four hours my life has been in turmoil. Yet it might help me later if I recollect and record my thoughts and emotions while events are still fresh in my mind.

In particular, I have long marvelled at how Jesus could simultaneously be not only our Master but also our Servant. I shall forever ponder on the conclusive evidence of that duality, which became manifest in our last extraordinary group supper together.

'Now, you all know that I am hosting our own private Passover meal in Jerusalem this evening. So, for fear of intervention by the authorities, I have arranged in secret to hire a large furnished upper room. To make the necessary final preparations, I need a couple of you to meet the owner's friend near Caiaphas's residence in the upper city, and be shown where it is. The man will be carrying a large water jar for identification,' explained Jesus. Clearly, he realised that his actions earlier in the week had put us all in increased danger, but I already sensed that his concern now was purely over the physical safety of us, his disciples and followers. Not his own.

Fortunately, the hustle and bustle of the packed city meant that we all managed to congregate without too much risk of detection that evening. We were looking forward above all to a convivial bonding get-together, along with the chance to hear about Jesus's inspiring plans for the rest of the week. Or so we thought. But what a bombshell right from the start.

His opening remarks before the main meal set the tone, as it confirmed my hunch that he no longer prioritised his personal well-being. Far from it. 'Tonight may well be a threshold occasion. In obedience to my Father's will, I am about to suffer. That is certain, because one of you here has agreed with my enemies to betray me.' No name was given, but I privately wondered why Judas Iscariot was straightaway protesting his innocence. As if he had read my thoughts, Jesus then broke bread and dipped it into a dish, giving a piece to Judas with a meaningful look. 'Do quickly what you are going to do.' What did that actually mean? No one was sure if there was a connection. After all, Judas held our common purse - buy something for the festival? give money to the poor? Only the two of them really understood exactly why Judas immediately slipped away.

That aside, the rest of us inevitably felt troubled by the sobering start to this special occasion. Nevertheless, I had no doubt that Jesus would move on to more familiar inspirational themes. Indeed, he immediately calmed everyone as he interceded again, breaking bread once more, with the words, 'Take, eat, this is my body.' And, giving thanks, he passed round the cup and said, 'This is my blood of a new covenant, which is poured out for many for the forgiveness of sins.' If the worst happened, was this the establishment of a ceremony by which we would always remember him in future?

Definitely no room for complacency by us, the eleven remaining disciples, though, because Jesus next proceeded to use even ever-supportive Peter to help make another point. Rising from the table, Jesus took off his outer garment and wrapped a towel round his waist. 'Yes, I am your Teacher, your Lord, but tonight I will wash your feet in humility. Stop vying with one another to be the greatest. Just serve one another as equals. Love one another as I have loved you.' And he proceeded to perform this meaningful gesture for us, one after another.

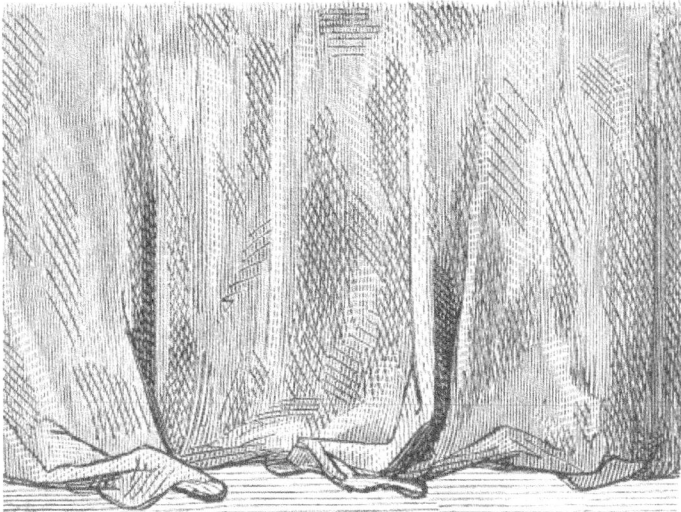

The Master taking on the role of Servant. However, when it came to Peter's turn, he impulsively started to protest, with his usual confused bluster. 'Your heart within may indeed be clean,' said Jesus, in response, 'but Satan challenges us all, including you. Before the cock crows, you will deny me thrice.' All very mysterious. 'Lord, I am ready to go with you to prison and death,' came Peter's instinctively fierce riposte. A rather embarrassing exchange, I felt, but powerful at so many levels.

So much more was to follow. Jesus returned to his place and proceeded to pay us the ultimate compliment. Almost as if in farewell thanks. 'You have stood by me in my trials, so I confer on you, just as my Father has conferred on me, a place at the kingdom table.' That assertion amazed us all. Virtually guaranteed that we disciples would redouble our efforts at spreading his good news, come what may.

But then the painful reality. 'I am with you only a little longer. Where I am going, you cannot come. For now. But fear not. I will prepare places for you in my Father's house.' Thomas looked particularly puzzled. I too had been listening intently, but in similar confusion I couldn't stop myself from blurting out, 'How can this be? Show us the Father.' 'Oh, Philip,' Jesus replied, disappointed in me. 'I am in the Father, and he is in me. So your future with him is guaranteed because you have known me...the way, the truth and the life.'

'Maybe, when I am gone, you will need another Advocate. In-dwelling, the Spirit of truth. And I assure you that this Sprit will also be available for everyone who keeps my commandments. You must all pass on that vital message.' And, showing his fundamental confidence in us, he proceeded to tell one of his inimitable parables. Himself as the vine, us as his branches, who as such will bear much fruit for the kingdom.

On any other occasion, utterly uplifting. But his message about parting from us was slowly sinking in. He knew, all too well. 'You will weep and mourn soon, but through you the world will rejoice. Your pain will turn into joy. Ask anything and you will receive,' he promised. However, he was realistic. He exhorted us to have courage, if necessary in the face of much future persecution. In that certainty came a bold statement, 'Together we will conquer the world!'

And he closed by looking up to heaven, knowing that the threshold to his time with us had been reached. Now had come the time for him to depart, in obedience to the Father. Time for the assembly to set off into the dark night, towards the Mount of Olives, to the Garden of Gethsemane to pray. In our exhaustion, to our shame, we fell asleep there. Then, awoken by torchlights and confusion, in the face of armed soldiers, all but Peter abandoned him.

And today, by cruel hands, his mortal body died on the cross. Pain personified. He is in God's hands now though, so something dramatic will surely happen very soon. Then we disciples will be called for. Put to the test. Inspired by these parting words of Jesus, 'Father, the world does not know you, but I know you and these know that you have sent me. The glory that you have given me I have given them. I ask you to protect them.'

The ensuing days and weeks will be desperate. But after all that was said at our last supper, I am sure that today's barbarous crucifixion is not the end. We disciples are a devoted group, to one another and to the cause. Above all, to the Servant King. Jesus will come again in glory, we are still convinced. He will never leave us, nor we him. Together transforming life on earth with his new vision.

Philip, a disciple of Jesus

Footnote

That Last Supper commemorated by Christians especially on Maundy Thursday of Easter week...the scriptural basis for the Eucharist.

The traditional location of the upper room is in an area that, according to archaeology, had a large Essene community.

Some modern scholars see the meal as a climax of a series of Messianic meals in anticipation of a new Exodus.

Leonardo da Vinci's depiction is considered the first work of High Renaissance art, due to its high level of harmony.

Pieces of Silver...

You probably haven't read a suicide note before. You can do so now, if you read on.

The sense of desolation is no one's fault but my own. I have let down myself, my friends and the one I held most dear. So how can I possibly go on with life? It's time to end it.

Yet I have just experienced the best three years of my life. I had a responsible position amongst new friends, in charge of keeping the group's common purse...I lapsed only a little, though hindsight is a harsh judge. We were having such an amazing influence on the well-being of the crowds who came to hear our remarkable leader, Jesus, even if some were slow to comprehend his message. No blame on them there actually. In fact, he often needed to go to great lengths to ensure that even we disciples could grasp it all. Gave us further tuition in private. Despite which, we rarely exuded flawless comprehension!

But increasingly I was becoming alarmed by the opposition we were encountering from the Jewish hierarchy. Not sure who, how or why exactly, but I knew their spies were being posted amongst the crowds, maybe even within our extended close followers. So I had reached as far as to fear for Jesus's life. What more could I do to protect him, I wondered? Hard to know, but I didn't dare share my worries with anyone else. Anyway, in the end my fellow disciples all seemed to be too carried away by the enthusiastic hysteria around Passover week, especially that early triumphal progress on a donkey, to look over-concerned.

But in the last few days the Roman authorities too seemed to be getting very threatening, fearing popular insurrection in Jerusalem. Admittedly, Jesus had been causing one or two scenes, but he was no rabble-rouser. So ironic that he should be perceived thus, as Jesus was not in any way the political zealot some of the masses had hoped for... in fact many were very disappointed. He was totally disinterested in earthly power. However, by now the Romans were watching us very closely, more likely to do him harm than even the Jewish priests might. Then, as it seemed to me, Jesus began to show definite signs of feeling so threatened that he himself was almost expecting to be killed. I freaked out, I suppose.

At that point I made my fatal misjudgment. I persuaded myself that Jesus would now be safer in Jewish than Roman hands. So, I thought…if I were to help the priests to capture him and keep him out of circulation for a few days, the Passover storm would blow over and the immediate crisis could be avoided. In secret the priests and I did a deal. Money wasn't the main aim but they did offer me a generous thirty pieces of silver.

Action at nighttime suited them best - less people to notice. I knew the ideal chance was imminent, following our next late meal in an upper room. But that night Jesus seemed to see straight through me, offering me a piece of dipped bread, with a significant stare and a few piercing words. Then, nevertheless, in effect further conspiring in his own fate by taking his disciples off to the Garden of Gethsemane. There I identified him to his potential captors with a kiss on the cheek…'Rabbi'. All so simple for a few of the High Priest's soldiers to arrest him, despite a bit of a struggle from one or two disciples. But most of them fled. For my part, I wept.

Too late, I realised that the opposition's collaboration behind the

scenes was greater than I had thought. They were all out to dispose of Jesus once and for all. Maybe even a crucifixion if it could be wangled. What a terrible fate, if so. And all my fault. In my self-disgust, I threw the coins to the floor next day in front of the priests, but they just sneered.

So, hours later, I have nowhere to turn. 'I have sinned by betraying innocent blood,' I keep thinking to myself, over and over. Maybe God will avenge by causing me to 'burst asunder', or maybe I will just hang myself. Either way, my only recourse is to leave this earth as quickly as possible - suicide. Clinging to my last, probably vain hope that Jesus will forgive me when he ascends to his Heavenly Father. At least I did understand his purposes and true identity better than most. Why, oh why, was I such a fool?

Judas Iscariot, a disciple of Jesus

Footnote

All in all, a huge paradox. Strange for such a betrayal to be the precursor to the salvation of mankind via the cross. Necessary and unavoidable, therefore, but leading to condemnation.

An introduction to the recently re-discovered Coptic 'Gospel of Judas' states that 'Christ's betrayer was his truest disciple'.

Another tradition has it that the priests used the money Judas returned to buy a field to bury strangers in, 'The Field of Blood'.

Innocent...

Over many generations, especially recently, my ancestors have done increasingly well in the world, especially considering our plebeian roots. Consular status has always been the ambitious family aim. And I think I have done my bit for our prestige in battling my way to the governorship of Judaea, by courtesy of Emperor Tiberius. All those corners I cut on the way up have been fully vindicated, I reckon. Pragmatic, I call it, though others have labelled it differently at times, I know. It worked for me. Time to consolidate myself here now, enjoy my status and treat myself to a bit of luxury. Nice big palace on the coast for a start. Reinforcing the town there as the focal point of all the administration, along with my military headquarters.

Unfortunately, those Jewish people can be a truculent lot. Ungrateful for the law and order I'm offering. Seem to forget that I renovated and expanded their Temple till it looked truly magnificent. Made a big fuss when I displayed the emperor's image on the banners of the legions. Well, why not? Not sure now if I was right to try and curry favour by letting them have their way again eventually. Devious and self-seeking some of their leaders are, for all their pious talk. I understand that. But I need them on my side. Good job it suits both parties to work together in order to maintain the status quo.

I remember one particular occasion that was especially tricky though. Actually, I tried not to get involved too much as I sensed complications might ensue. It was the annual Jewish Passover in Jerusalem, so I had been obliged to travel there with a goodly number of troops in case the usual huge influx of people caused chaos and fomented dissent. A show of military force can have a big calming effect, I always find. Deploying enough troops to nip problems in the bud.

However, that year one particular itinerant maverick from up north had been causing trouble from day one of Passover with some sort of minor but noisy procession. Ludicrous, with just an ass and a colt, and a few palm branches. Of course, not a patch on the awe my troops can

instantly inspire when they are massed together in their disciplined ranks. Then he outraged my collaborators amongst the Jewish leaders who were helping me to keep order, by creating mayhem in the Temple, of all places. Turned over the money-changers' tables, I was told. In the end I was persuaded to let their officers lead a cohort of my men and its tribune to effect his arrest one night. I think they hoped that would start to solve things, fearing that I might lose my patience with the whole lot of them otherwise. Too right.

But it was only stage one. They really wanted to seize this chance to get rid of him once and for all. They first took him to the house of Annan, father-in-law of Caiaphas, the chief priest who was masterminding the situation. The troublemaker, Jesus by name, was so disrespectful to them that he was soon taken for further interrogation by me outside the Praetorium.

Even I was a little surprised by all their fury and determination. 'Only you can authorise his death,' they said, quite correctly. I was a bit rattled, so I took Jesus inside for a private questioning. The leading accusation they wanted me to pin on him was over a political claim to be King of the Jews. That he only meant it in an other-worldly sense was the worst I could get him to confess to. Something about truth, but I couldn't follow him. Went right over my head. Thankfully, all that was not a problem for me to address. 'You will have to deal with him yourselves,' I adjudicated. 'Or I can release him as a Passover gesture.' Yet, so obsessed were they that they preferred me to release instead a definitely dangerous bandit called Barabbas. That shows you.

This whole situation would have been tricky enough at a purely secular or law and order level. But having a wife who is a proselyte to Judaism was making everything even harder for me. My Claudia, being a granddaughter of the Emperor Augusutus, has been very helpful behind the scenes in my career, I have to admit, so ignoring her completely is never an option. Having insisted on accompanying me here to Jerusalem is testament to her persuasive powers over me, I suppose, as most husbands would have refused such a demand. Anyway, like so many before her, she seemed rather to have fallen for this prisoner…from a safe distance, at least. So maybe I shouldn't have been surprised when she tried to intercede with me on his behalf. 'Have nothing to do with condemning him. He's a just man. I've had a message to that effect in a rather troubled dream,' she pleaded with me, in a hurried little note. I sympathised, deep down. But clearly, though I had tried to explain the side issues, she didn't properly understand. Or didn't want to.

At least it encouraged me to try prevaricating further. As a result, off the Jewish leaders went to see if they could get a better decision out of Herod who was quite close by in Jerusalem. He was delighted at the chance to mock their victim and tried to engage him in conversation. To no avail. So he too got nowhere and sent him and his guards on their way. Passing the buck back to me then.

To be honest, I was getting exasperated. The usual scourging seemed finally in order, then mockery from my soldiers. In his case, a few personal touches got added. Twisting thorns into a painfully sharp wreath and crowning him with it. A purple robe round his shoulders. Quick slap on the face and a hissed 'Hail, King of the Jews'. Then parading him back to his countrymen. 'Blasphemy. Crucify him,' the accusers immediately retorted. And a little baying crowd echoed the demand, spurred on by a few of their 'plants', I shouldn't wonder. Such hate, such spite, though personally I hadn't found much wrong with him really. But he wouldn't stand up for himself properly. Worse, he told me I had no authority over him. Answerable only to his God. Maintained he was superior to all his accusers. I had had enough of him. The end.

Technically innocent, as far as I was concerned. That remained a big dilemma. Secretly, I still agreed with my wife. But then the priests

started to play up big time. Said they would report me to Emperor Caesar for sticking up for this rival king. It wasn't worth risking that, so I handed him over. To whatever fate awaited him now. Literally washed my hands of him. Well, he wouldn't be the first Jew to be crucified on flimsy charges. That was definitely the best practical solution. Bit of rough justice, allied to cruelty, never did any harm in showing who's boss...such a successful policy for me until then. I was just relieved to think he was probably going off to Golgotha and that would finally be the end of all this nonsense. Sadly, subsequent events seem to be proving how badly I had misjudged the obstinacy of his deluded followers.

Pontius Pilate, governor of Judaea

Footnote

The fate of Pontius Pilate is unclear. One tradition says suicide to avoid the wrath of the new emperor Caligula for continuing incompetence. Another that his body was thrown into the river Tiber and washed up at Vienna!

However, a third says he became a Christian, (maybe his wife too), such that some Eastern Churches regard him as a martyr/ saint!

The trial and its tribulations are woven into Bulgakov's Master and Margarita parable/novel.

And Turner immortalised his most famous act in art, via his Pilate Washing his Hands.

A Burden Shared...

So many of us Jews are living away from our homeland in communities scattered far and wide across the Roman Empire. With differing degrees of prosperity. Actually, though, in my case Cyrene offers a more than satisfactory lifestyle day-to-day. Originally, it was established In the heyday of Greek influence a few centuries ago as a place of resettlement. Blessed with many impressive marks of their cultured ways. Just a few kilometres from the coast on the southern side of the Mediterranean in a fertile area around a spring. Today, a settled metropolis of about 5,000, with assorted shrines, temples and baths - enough facilities to suit everyone. Famed as a centre of philosophical debate, but with plenty of scope for the large Jewish representation to flourish in our own unique way, worshipping the one true God…as long as we continue to behave ourselves. Yes, the usual problem of ultimate Roman control over everyone, in what has become a disciplined centre of local administration.

That apart, my life runs smoothly. Though you won't be surprised to hear that for many of us the highlight will always be the lengthy pilgrimage to the annual Passover week in Jerusalem. We Jewish Cyrenians are sufficient in number to have established our own synagogue there, in which I am often honoured to play a leading role during those celebrations. Distinguished, I would immodestly claim, to such an extent that I am known to Jews all around the city as Simon of Cyrene.

However, this year Passover has been far from straightforward. What an understatement! I am still traumatised by what happened yesterday. Getting accidentally sucked into the mistreatment of one of my fellow Jews. Admittedly, his activities in recent months had already been getting under the skin of our pious religious leaders, and so they were on the lookout for him this week. Of course, he and his followers from Galilee had every right to simply enjoy the celebrations with us all, but he seems deliberately to have exacerbated matters by some provocative activities. Starting with a symbolic ride into the city on a donkey, from the Bethany direction. Followers singing, 'Hosanna. Blessed is he who comes in the name of the Lord.' The militant Messiah some are looking for, perhaps? Reinforcing the possibility since by continually stirring up the crowds with charismatic preaching and teaching, even claiming some sort of intimate affinity with God himself, according to the gossip going round. Some reckon it's really blasphemous. Perhaps it was only to be expected that all our authority figures would want to find a way to nail him…literally, in the end, it has transpired!

Rumours abound over what happened behind closed doors to pave the way for his demise. Somehow, in a final dismissive decision, either in his own quarters or at Gabbatha in front of the Praetorium, Pilate was reluctantly persuaded to condemn the man to death. Whatever the rights and wrongs, that terrible victim's trudge to Golgotha inevitably ensued - no doubt after a little initial debilitating rough stuff from his Roman captors. The crowds en route were by now mostly baying against this Jesus…presumably any of his actual original supporters were just cowering in the background, if still around at all, for fear of their own arrest. So those brutal Roman soldiers goaded him along the packed noisy streets, pushed and shoved him as he struggled under the strain of carrying the heavy wooden cross piece that would form part of his own crucifixion ordeal.

I was there to witness this increasingly cruel stage. No, much more than that, I must explain. To actually take part - against my will, of course. It was all awful, but I was mesmerised. Somehow feeling drawn towards him in an overwhelming sense of helplessness as his staggering progress got slower and slower. I didn't know him personally, yet my spirit yearned to assist. He looked so physically spent. And, as a result, I incautiously got a little too close for my own good. I guess the soldiers had begun to fear he might expire before reaching the destination, depriving the mob of their spectator sport. Seeking to alleviate the problem, one of them looked round for a different sort of victim. He grabbed me, before I could realise his intentions. Roughly shoved me to the man's side and ordered me to take over carrying the wooden beam. Suddenly, as I brushed against this Jesus, an extraordinary spark went through me. And the look of love on that fellow Jew's face I will never forget. Otherworldly, despite his pain and exhaustion. Whispered that he was going to his Father, and promising that we would meet again there. A claim to be nothing less than the son of God, in other words. Not blasphemous. A revelation. I truly believed him. Still do.

Relieved of his weighty burden, his demeanour and gait improved a little. I followed, close behind. Bitterly resenting what I was being forced to do. But both of us were instantly manhandled by the soldiers if ever we faltered. Even spat upon too by some in the crowd lining the streets. Until finally Golgotha loomed in front of us, and another soldier grasped the beam from me. Three crosses in all were being prepared, and, recoiling from the ultimate horrors to come, I'm ashamed to say that I started to melt away, scared in case the bloodlust might spread to bring further mistreatment on me too. The extra soldiers at the crucifixion site were in an equally evil mood, mocking him afresh. I couldn't bear to watch this good man die. However that little band of womenfolk were managing to stay at the scene, close to the agony, I will never know. Seemingly prepared to watch and weep to the very end. I wasn't.

Of course, it has all totally ruined Passover for me. This morning, depressed but out and about again after a sleepless troubled night, I felt physically sick as I encountered others still celebrating, blissfully unaware of the latest example of the barbarity that surrounds us. I wonder how his inner band of followers are feeling now, wherever they are hiding. I have just overheard a couple of folk in the street talking of unprecedented claims he would be resurrected. Soon, they say. Seems farfetched. But then I remembered. Despite only having met him briefly in violent circumstances, I had undeniably sensed that this leader was indeed special. Something extraordinary is more than possible.

Whatever am I going to tell them in the synagogue?

Simon of Cyrene

═Footnote═

Ironically, tradition says that, in AD 100, Simon of Cyrene was martyred by crucifixion - and cut in half by a saw.

Again, that his later life had been spent in Egypt, sharing the gospel.

Possibly following in his missionary footsteps were his sons, Alexander and Rufus.

In the Sixties film, The Greatest Story Ever Told, Simon of Cyrene was played by Sidney Poitier.

Three times...

Will I be able to cope? What did he see in me? But Jesus has gone now. Just as he predicted. To be with his Father. And left me in charge on earth...or so it feels to me. Just a bluff fisherman called Simon, but for three years I have been proud to bear the nickname he gave me - Cephas, Peter, the Rock. At the time, during his ministry, I was pleased that it conferred on me a tacit authority over the other disciples. And I responded by often taking the lead.

Unfortunately, on too many occasions for my liking, I overreached myself. Bit too keen and impetuous. Out to prove myself to him. Impress the other disciples too. Like the time I thought I could walk on water. 'O, thou of little faith!' he said as I faltered. All rather humiliating. Though on the other hand, I was the first one to recognise that he was the Son of God. For once I was truly happy with myself for something. That perception left me feeling reassured and affirmed.

It didn't last long, however. A week, in fact, before I again felt out of my depth. Typical of the oftentimes when he chose me, perhaps with James or John, for certain special occasions. This one maybe the most notable, inviting us to escort him up to the mountaintop to pray together. There to witness a unique moment as the transfigured face of Jesus shone like the sun. In which guise, discoursing with the apparitions of Moses and Elijah. A magic fulfilment of so much prophesy, I felt. However...trust me to lower the tone with one of my crass suggestions, offering to make three tents for them! Luckily, no less than the voice of God suddenly distracted us all, 'This is my beloved son, with whom I am well pleased; listen to him.' We three disciples, in further shock, certainly needed a subsequent calming touch from Jesus. Though his demand to keep everything secret till he was raised from the dead added another conundrum to our confusion at that stage. As we descended, so many questions thereby inevitably remaining unasked, and in the aftermath. Only now can I dare to grasp the full significance.

For other situations too, a dozen of us was an inappropriately large number. How humbling, consistently to be one of his hand-picked chosen few from the larger group. For example, when accompanying him into Jairus's house under very stressful circumstances. Or being sent on ahead to fetch the ass and colt for that triumphant ride into Jerusalem at the beginning of this latest Passover week.

Or, even more recently, going further than most of the other disciples into the Garden of Gethsemane, preparing with Jesus for a crucial evening of prayer, with so much threat all around. To my everlasting regret, though, I then failed to stay awake, even just for an hour, fully deserving yet another of those habitual rebukes. So you won't find it surprising when I confess to reacting with my usual over compensation. Seeing Judas identifying him to the guards in betrayal, I rushed to intervene, trying to save him. Finished up by wildly cutting off someone's ear in the process! Of course, Jesus, after chastising me once more, ignored his personal danger, took pity on the man, touched the injured spot and healed him. Typical. Anyway, as for myself, it was clearly reckless, and all in vain. It just made me a marked man.

Which brings me to my most irresolute moments of all. The worst of
it is that Jesus had predicted everything about me beforehand at supper.
Told me I would deny him thrice before the cock would crow. Of course,
I protested vehemently. I was his Rock after all. 'I will never disown
you.' But it happened. Stage by stage, before I quite realised it.

From the garden they had dragged him off to the house of the High
Priest's father-in-law. I surreptitiously followed with one of the other
disciples who knew his way around there and he managed to get the
girl on duty to let me in to the courtyard as well. But, while doing so,

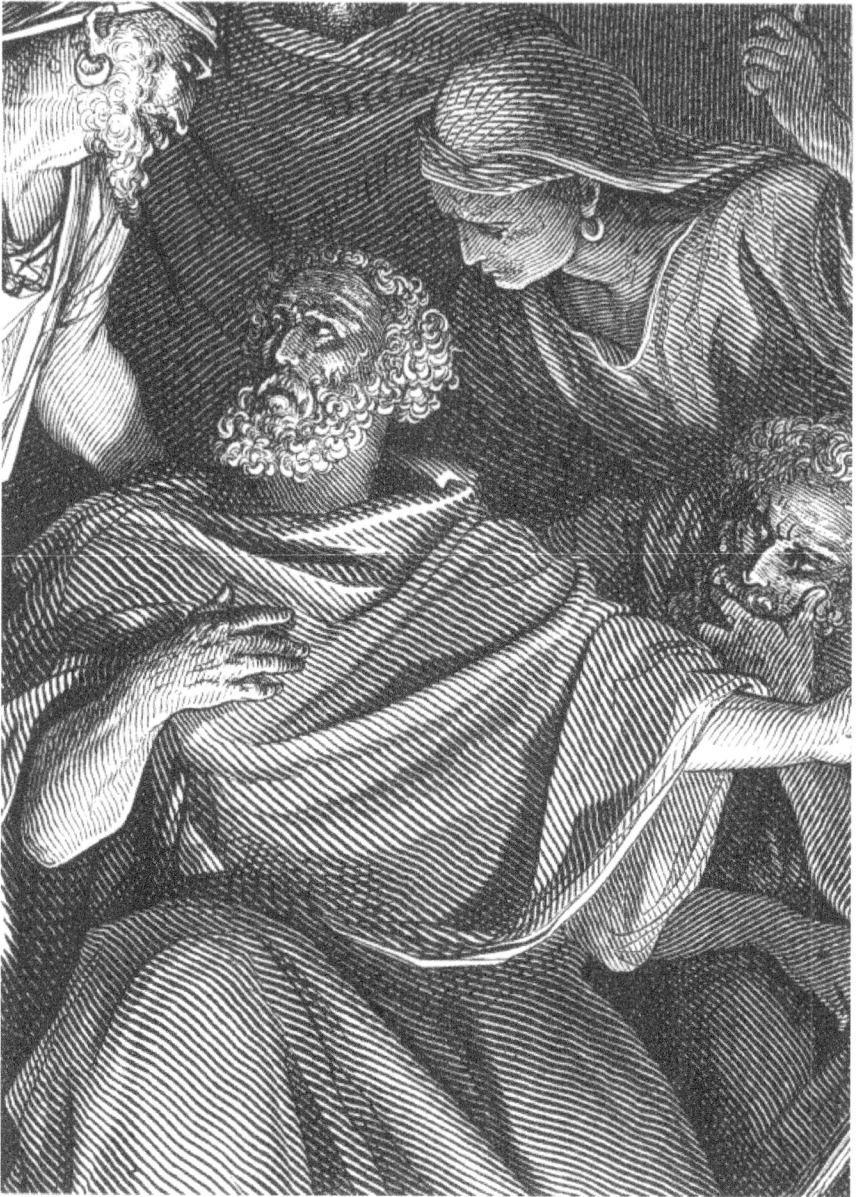

she stared hard at me and burst out, 'This man was with him.' 'Not a chance,' I replied. But a little while later, looking even more intently by the light of a charcoal fire, she persisted, this time saying in the hearing of the others round about, 'This fellow was with him.' What choice did I have? Surely, before things got nasty, I had to say, 'I was not.' And then, an even more dangerous moment as one of the servants, a relative of the man whose ear I had cut off, challenged me. 'Didn't I see you in the olive grove with him? And I recognise your accent. You're certainly a Galilean too.' An instant rebuttal was my only chance. And I'd hardly uttered it when the rooster crowed. And I remembered the Lord's words. In utter disgust with myself, I sneaked off and wept outside, bitterly.

That subsequent terrible crucifixion ordeal is too painful to recount. I still hurt so much. Haven't managed to process it all yet. Suffice to say, we all knew that Joseph of Arimathea, a follower but in secret for fear of his reputation, had got permission to place the body in his tomb, guarded nonetheless by Roman soldiers. But the next morning Mary Magdalene couldn't keep away, in all her hysterical grief. Amazed at finding the tomb empty, with the huge entrance stone rolled away, she dashed back to tell us, so John and I set off. He is younger and fitter than I am, so got there first, but hesitated in temporary fear. But I was my usual impetuous self and entered. To see just strips of linen and a separate head cloth. No body. He promised, I know, but had he really been raised from the dead? Despair turned into hope, then into belief and new found resolution. I prayed hard. Time to return to the others, embolden them and make plans. In the future, be that Rock Jesus always intended me to be. Especially when Mary, who had lingered, came back with claims she had personally met the resurrected Lord. Who had promised to meet us all again soon in Galilee, alongside my beloved lake.

Simon Peter, a disciple of Jesus

Footnote

Shamed but then re-commissioned after a lakeside breakfast Resurrection appearance by Jesus, Peter was galvanized.

In authority in Jerusalem, he performed miracles and undertook missionary journeys. In later years, his dramatic activities imperilled his life. Arrested, he was freed from prison by an angel. He went to Rome and was probably martyred there, crucified upside-down.

Great artists painted many scenes in his life...Raphael, Rembrandt, Michelangelo, etc. Sculptors and painters identify him by placing in his hands the emblematic crossed keys.

HERE HANGS A MAN DISCARDED...

Suppression...

Every year I really relish our annual trip out to Jerusalem. It's enjoyable doing my bit to keep those unruly Jews in order when they all gather from far and wide to celebrate their Passover week. They are a strange lot. I quite see why they hate us Romans lording it over them. But then they should be used to it. Their whole history is riddled with disaster as a nation. They just seem to have been perpetual victims. Occasionally, the odd hero emerges to give them hope. Telling them that their solo God is all powerful and this time he will lead them to a promised land, flowing with milk and honey and the like. But it never lasts long and they soon slide back into their usual submissive role.

Admittedly, we Roman military are so well disciplined they don't have much chance to be otherwise these days. And they are hardly the only ones. None of the other countries around have much choice either, though some of their tough guys always switch to our side and have a nice life in our soldier ranks. Seeing the world sometimes. Actually, the cleverest idea is how our bosses just find a few key local bigwigs, then bribe or reward them well and give them a modicum of power. Works a treat. Take the case of Herod the Great, as some call him. We popped him on the throne of Judaea as a client king and let him get on with it, under our supervision, of course. He loved the grandeur of all those building projects. Some of it was to keep the Jews sweet, sort of. Sadly, lots of them have always been ungrateful, though, however much is done for them. In his time, Herod gave them lots to be proud of. Rebuilding their Temple in Jerusalem and expanding the Temple Mount towards the north. Remember the enclosure project around the caves of the Patriarchs in Hebron. And what about Herodium, admittedly built mainly for his own glory, but still an impressive new town with its wonderful palaces and pleasure grounds! Then those other extra palaces when he strengthened the fortress at Masada. Above all maybe, after we gave him the old site at Caesarea Maritima, he spared no expense on the new harbour, on building wide roads, baths, temples, public buildings and so on. I particularly admire the spectacle round those gladiator games of his. Of course, we've more recently made it the civil and military capital instead of Jerusalem, and doesn't old Pontus Pilate now enjoy living there! Anyway, I'm rambling on too much. The point is, the Jews do love Jerusalem still, flocking for Passover, so we have a duty to temporarily reinforce our strength and keep them under control.

Usually it's straightforward. We extra soldiers march in from our coastal base, looking intimidating, hand out a few punishments, and Passover passes off smoothly, even if a trifle chaotically. However, this year was a bit trickier. Some of the yokels, from up north especially, have a new hero. I know he doesn't dare have military aspirations, though some of them want him to be a bolshy Messiah figure. No, he is cleverer than that. He made a gesture, riding into town on a donkey… symbolic to them, I suppose, but pretty feeble really. And it all started to rattle their two-timing priests again, who felt that their responsibility to us Romans might be undermined, as well as worrying about the risk of losing their pampered status. So they got the prefect to let them engineer his crucifixion. Not a big deal. We've crucified thousands of others in the past and routinely still do. But this time I was on duty there myself, so naturally it all seemed a bit special somehow. Maybe I'm going soft, but I warmed to him as the main victim of the three we nailed up

together on that occasion. Anyway, I helped do the usual, with a few extra trimmings that seemed to apply to this man's situation. Stripped him naked, flogged him across the back, buttocks and legs with a lot of bleeding. Cast lots for his garments. Taunted him as he tried to carry the crosspiece out to Golgotha. Fixed him to a post, with a crown of thorns on his head, and put up a King of the Jews sign to remind everyone that's what happens if you make bogus claims. Pretty unedifying close up, it has to be said. And all that wailing from the womenfolk made it seem worse.

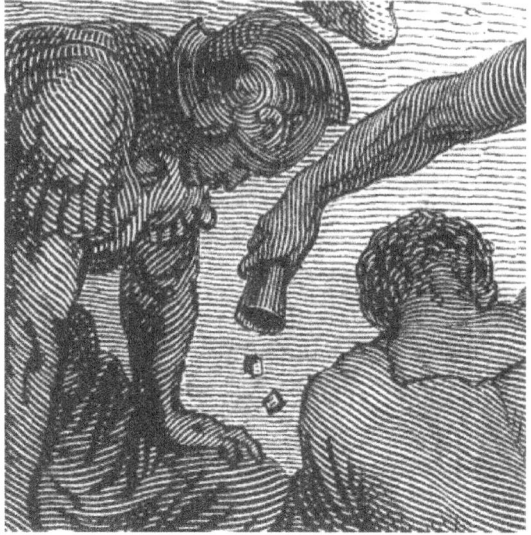

But I hate to admit it…the man was very dignified and impressive, considering the agonising circumstances. So we put a spear in his side, to help him to an early death. And I was pleased actually when I saw one of his own had secured permission to take the body reverently down and take it off to a specially prepared local sepulchre. Fair enough, as a one off. But here's the thing. Maybe we should learn a lesson because that leniency seems to have created extra problems for us. Some of my colleagues were posted to guard the tomb overnight, with its big stone at the entrance. And they are now in such big disciplinary trouble for sleeping on the job. They claim someone must have given them some drugged wine. Perhaps so, but I gather a few of the dead man's most ardent followers are now claiming a miracle has occurred. As if a lowly criminal would merit any such thing. But his body has certainly disappeared, so they reckon he has been resurrected. Apparently, they insist he predicted it! Sounds fraudulent to me, but that's not my problem. I'm more bothered about the slur on our reputation as efficient soldiers. I have a feeling we all haven't got to the bottom of this, in more ways than one.

Roman soldier at the crucifixion

=Footnote=

Crucifixion most likely began with the Assyrians and the Babylonians, continuing with the Persians, and it was brought back to the Eastern Mediterranean by Alexander the Great, but initially just using a tree or post without the crosspiece, a later Roman refinement.

In 4BC the Roman general Varus crucified 2,000 Jews in one purge, and mass crucifixions continued throughout the first century AD. For slaves, disgraced soldiers, Christians, foreigners and particularly political activists.

Penitence...

Forgive me, but I won't record my name - it's unimportant anyway - in case this note falls into the wrong hands. For fear my sympathies and associations are punished. Nevertheless, don't doubt my testimony, however incredible it seems.

I so wish it were different, but today one of my best friends died, horribly. Crucified, hanging from nails on a crude cross. One of those thousands of barbaric wooden backdrops on which many a body has been tortured in agony and humiliation on the way to a lingering death. All too effective in achieving the hated Romans' purpose to intimidate local populations throughout the Empire over which they rule with a rod of iron.

The whole sordid episode I observed in horror from the sidelines. About my friend I had been worrying for weeks, and especially in the last few days as the noose tightened. I reckon someone must have betrayed him. In the dead of night a gang of soldiers laid rough hands on him and marched him away. Actually, I assumed the inevitable crucifixion would be a routine affair today, Friday. Then I learned he was to be hung alongside two other unfortunates who had displeased the authorities. Outside the city gates on Golgotha, the place of skulls. The very name makes me shudder. Not somewhere I wanted my friend Dismas to die. A criminal maybe, but to me mostly just a loveable rogue.

However, one of the other victims had been actively stirring up trouble during this Passover week. Encouraged by hundreds of supporters from out of town. Creating a scene in the Temple by overturning the money changers' tables. Making preposterous claims, I gather. Understandably upsetting Roman and Jewish leaders alike. Until finally the chief priests and scribes managed to trick Pilate and Herod into condemning him to death - even if it meant sparing the notorious Barabbas in the process. Well, this week's trouble maker was only a Galilean. What did his followers expect?

Actually, unlike in my friend's situation, the Romans initially tried to make this Jesus carry his own cross. Totally unreasonable, even in his case, especially through such narrow streets, lined with a mixture of jeerers and cheerers. In the end, one of the sicarii, Simon of Cyrene, was forced to carry it for him most of the way. And even when they had him virtually nailed up on the cross, the soldiers wouldn't leave him alone. Temporarily dressed him in a seamless purple robe, before eventually casting lots for all his clothes. Put a cruel crown of thorns on his head. Affixed a mocking sign 'This is the King of the Jews'. At the last, offered him sour vinegar on a sponge. Pierced his side with a spear. Unpalatable stuff, indeed.

And, adding insult to injury, Gestas, the third sufferer on the cross to his left, challenged him to save all three of them and prove he was the Messiah, as his followers claimed. Provocative. But here's the remarkable thing. This Jesus behaved regally throughout. Crying out to his absent father in agony...yes. But somehow dignified, and certainly selfless. Proved when, despite his own plight, he showed camaraderie and compassion to my friend hanging on his right. A repentant Dismas, with an extraordinary flash of insight, asked to be remembered when Jesus arrived in his kingdom...and that wish was mercifully granted. Penitence rewarded. Nevertheless, I found it remarkable how even the grieving women, exhausted and helpless at the foot of his cross, didn't look surprised at the outcome of that exchange.

If I'm honest, my friend and the other thief deserved to die. But the man in the middle...no way. He transcended that awful, earthly scene. And then - unprecedented in the dozens of other crucifixions I have witnessed - it was as if the elements wanted to get involved. The face of the sun disappeared. The sky went prematurely black for a terrifying three hours. I have since heard rumours that the veil of the Temple was torn in two as Jesus gave up the ghost. And the earth did quake and the rocks rent. It was as if - because his time on earth was about to end - the end was imminent for the whole of mankind too. But instead, perhaps it all marked a new beginning?

I couldn't bear to stay till the nasty aftermath. Helpless on behalf of my friend, I decided to slink away. But I've just been told that a rich sympathiser, Joseph of Arimathea, pleaded for Jesus' body. Most unorthodox. Wanted to wrap it in fine linen and lay it reverently in a quiet, nearby sepulchre. Actually, a dignity he fully deserved, I reckon. A final resting place? I wonder.

It looks like being a sad weekend ahead, but I'm already beginning to question what it all meant. After everything that happened today, I have a feeling we haven't heard the last of that Jesus. Even now, some still say he was the Son of God! I certainly won't ever forget him. In fact, I think I just might be coming to believe in him too.

An observer of the crucifixion

Footnote

The clash of secular politics with religious sensitivities is nowhere more exemplified than in Jesus's final Passover week. The Romans needed to get rid of him for disrupting the peace; religious leaders feared his threat to their authority; God's longer term plan rode on the back of those very parochial clashes.

Another beloved disciple?...

A weekend that changed my world, maybe everyone's. How devastated I felt on the Friday to witness, within touching distance, such an excruciating ordeal and horrifying spectacle on Golgotha. Mystified to believe such suffering could be justified. Or ever redeemed. But mere days later, in gradual recovery, I recall the personal preparation I had received beforehand from Jesus, so that I am not wholly surprised to have since encountered the early stages of a miraculous outcome.

During our many intimate conversations, Jesus had gradually unfolded his unique mission and identity to me. Fully human indeed, as the kisses we exchanged demonstrated, but also fully divine, as begotten by the will of God. His closest confidante on earth, I thereby experienced and consequently appreciated his inner life more than anyone else. A bold claim, I know.

His twelve male disciples had become utterly devoted as they too witnessed his miracles, parables, teachings and healings. But they somehow never anticipated the rocky path ahead that was slowly, almost imperceptibly, unwinding, however much an exasperated Jesus repeatedly tried to explain. All too human. Their frailties were similarly exhibited, with Peter always reckoning to be the most trustworthy, James and John jostling for top spot, Judas suddenly and devastatingly betraying him to his captors. Good men basically, but never really comprehending. Now they are about to face the ultimate challenge beyond the days of Jesus's earthly ministry.

In their male pride, will they be happy to acknowledge my female intuition and insight? Allow me to share what Jesus taught me one to one. I realise that they were uneasy from the start when he cast out the seven demons from me, cleansing me from my past terrors, then swept me increasingly into his companionship. I realise too that they

resented my extravagance in bathing his feet with my tears and hair, and anointing them with precious oils. Martha never understood either. Though Jesus clearly told her, 'It is Mary who has chosen the better part, and it is not to be taken from her.' Because by then I had discerned Jesus's imminent fate. And, despite others' doubts, he willingly accepted that my personal expression of an earthly farewell was appropriate. Our bond was that special.

However, no emotional, practical, intellectual, or even spiritual, preparation could lessen my despair at the foot of that barbaric cross. Being alongside my namesake Mary, his mother, made the grief even more intense. How ironic that we women, having less to fear than the male disciples from his Roman persecutors, were able to remain weeping all the closer to his agony. Small consolation afterwards that Joseph of Arimathea was permitted to receive the body down from the cross and tenderly remove it to a private sepulchre we all knew about nearby.

I make no apology for having allowed the brutality of the ordeal to blind me temporarily to God's plan, to forget what Jesus had taught me. But by the third day I was feeling ambivalent. Before any of the men were up, I rushed to the tomb early in the morning. Of course, I expected it still to be blocked by a huge boulder but I had come prepared at least to anoint the body if the opportunity arose. What a shock to find the stone rolled away. My heart leapt. Jesus had told me many times that his human death would not be the end, merely a precursor to a glorious redemption. Did this unexpected development somehow herald the new beginning, I wondered? I peered into the tomb. Nothing at first, then in the gloom I spied neatly folded grave clothes. Stunned again, I backed away. And suddenly sensed a presence nearby. A gardener? Actually, no. Overwhelmingly, I was feeling the spirit of Jesus, but not in a tangible sense. 'I am not yet risen to the Father' came the intuitive message. I knew the menfolk would find all this difficult to hear from me but, as in

his earthly life, so in this transition and for the beckoning future, I had again been chosen as the most blessed of his followers. The first with the revelation, with the life changing news. Privileged to become the apostle to the apostles.

Mary Magdalene, a follower of Jesus

Footnote

Maybe it is taking a liberty to elide the various 'clues' into one character but Mary Magdalene is a controversial figure in biblical scholarship.

The four gospels all display traces of her special relationship with Jesus. The Gnostic writings go much further, giving females a greater role in discipleship and acknowledging Mary's preeminence amongst them.

In the Gospel of Thomas a slightly envious Peter says, 'Sister, we know that the Teacher loved you differently from other women. Tell us whatever you remember of any words he told you which we have not heard'.

All remarkable in the cultural context of early Christianity.

WE GIVE
IMMORTAL PRAISE...

Only a mother...

The worst day of my life. A mother's suffering for her dear son, watching him die in agony on a rough Roman cross. Hard to credit that all my hopes for him were meant to end like that. My baby, like no other, the angel had told me. I cast my mind back over a few of the key moments since then. Starting some thirty years ago.

Newly betrothed, I thought I had everything safely prepared for a traditional future with a loving husband. But then my life changed irrevocably overnight with that mind blowing visitation from an angel, announcing my son's unique conception through the Holy Spirit. I was such a very young girl, yes, rather naive. And hardly reassured by that humble and unorthodox birth in a Bethlehem stable/cave, followed by the panicky flight from Herod's wrath.

An overwhelming responsibility from the start then, undiminished in the coming years as I strove to nurture that son Jesus's precocious childhood. He never seemed like other boys. Then moving on into his mature years, disputing and teaching in and outside the synagogue. So, forewarned and reminded throughout his upbringing, I was always aware that my eldest son was destined for service to his Heavenly Father…an unusual life has certainly unfolded, to say the very least.

But in so many ways he was also the perfect conventional human firstborn. Any mother's ideal. My husband, Joseph, doted on him too, despite initially needing reassurance during all the mystery over Jesus's divine paternity. He was thrilled to groom him in all the carpentry and building skills that underpinned the business that secured our family lifestyle. Yet, on that other level, to be honest we both struggled to come to terms with the persistent flashbacks that kept nagging at the back of our minds. We knew we were missing something.

I particularly remember our bizarre family visit to Jerusalem to celebrate Passover in the year of his coming of age. He made a big impression amongst his elders there alright, but early on the journey home we suddenly realised he wasn't with us. We rushed back, panicking for his safety in that crowded city. We roamed the streets, then realised he might still be in the Temple. Sure enough, deep in debate. He brushed off our concerns. Told us we should have come to understood him better by now. 'I must be in my Father's house' was the dismissive phrase he used. I didn't dare ask Joseph whether that ambiguous reminder made him personally feel just a little humiliated.

On Joseph's death, however, Jesus selflessly accepted his new responsibilities as male head of the family. Until finally, at the age of thirty, with all his siblings safely into adulthood, he began to cut himself free to embark on the challenge he had always felt called to confront. In some ways his like-minded cousin John was the crucial catalyst. Baptising in the River Jordan was the draw that initially attracted the crowds, and Jesus himself underwent a dramatic experience there which confirmed to them both God's blessing and pleasure at their emerging activities. From then on, Jesus's focus moved ever further away from us to embrace a much more complex itinerant lifestyle involving the wider community. Not exactly risk free, as any mother would feel.

Ironically, however, the first inkling of Jesus's miraculous powers had involved me. Just after he had added Philip and Nathaniel to his disciples, Jesus and I were invited to a relative's wedding at Cana. A lengthy occasion as ever, such that embarrassingly the wine began to run out. Naturally, I turned to Jesus for inspiration. 'Woman, what concern is that to you and me?' was his hardly encouraging initial response. But then, to my astonishment, he asked a waiter to fill some huge containers with water and take a small tasting to the chief steward. It made me smile that the bridegroom, all unaware, got the plaudits. 'Amazing and congratulations, but I don't understand why you have served the best wine last!' said the steward.

However, an apparent disastrous turn of events happened soon afterwards. Everything had been going so well. Despite some of the cousins' peers being dubious and shocked by the scale of unorthodox fervour in these two well-known locals, increasingly huge crowds flocked to follow their inspirational leadership. Then, John fell into Herod's clutches. I find it difficult to recall his cruel death…his severed head being paraded on a platter. Awful.

I thought this might completely paralyse Jesus, but, not for the first time, I underestimated him. How could I have so badly misjudged my own son's determination? Incredibly, he simply seemed to redouble his efforts. With now a dozen special disciples and a wider entourage of supporters, including some of his female friends, he soon attracted even more folk from far and wide to hear his teaching. He had a brilliant way with words. Those memorable parables especially. All underpinned by dramatic healing powers that staggered everyone. Was some of it down to my nurture as well as to his inherited nature, I wondered?

Though as family we saw him from time to time, we weren't really involved much in public from then on. But as a mother I naturally began to worry about the threat to his life this all might entail, not just from the Roman authorities but also from the Scribes and Pharisees who saw their influence over the people being undermined, along with a threat to the privileges they enjoyed from the Romans in exchange for acting as first line of defence in keeping the peace. So unnecessary, because Jesus never had any intention of seeking temporal power…his motives were far too devout and humble and eternal for that.

Of course, however much I felt initially that he had been tricked into provoking his own lingering cruel death, I was beginning to believe his insistence that it was essential for the salvation of humankind. Nevertheless, I can't find words adequately to portray my maternal suffering, then and still now, from watching my beloved son's horrendous crucifixion. Whipped, stripped, mocked, naked. All heightened by the weeping presence there of some of my dearest friends. In truth, however empathetic others were, only a mother could truly feel his pain. I will never forget that searing mix of blazing anger and intense agony as I

lay helplessly at the foot of that rough wooden torturing cross. My own precious flesh and blood…sacrificed, like a lamb. But how typical, at the height of his agony on the cross, that he found time to look at his beloved disciple John and turn to me, saying 'Woman, here is your son.' The ultimate in unselfish thoughtfulness.

Yet amazingly, Joseph of Arimathea's mysteriously empty sepulchre has indeed confirmed Jesus's claims that he would be resurrected on the third day to be with his Heavenly Father. And I have since been with his disciples in hiding recently and I am so impressed by their confidence and determination to carry on with the work.

Personally, I am convinced that the angel's promises to me from the start about my unique son are all coming true. During his time on earth, Jesus loved me deeply but perhaps always felt disappointed that I couldn't grasp the import of his full identity. But I do now. His Heavenly Father's will is finally unfolding.

Mary, the mother of Jesus

Footnote

The Blessed Virgin Mary, the Madonna, St Mary. Beyond her humanity, Christian doctrine has variously ascribed much veneration to Mary's role in the faith. An immaculate conception; a virgin holy mother of God; a second Eve; an assumption into Heaven; etc. 'Surely, from now on all generations shall call me blessed.'

In Islam too she holds the highest position amongst women.

Of great cultural significance…in feasts, devotional services, the Rosary, and a huge range of worldwide sacred art and literature throughout the centuries.

Seven miles home...

I can only think I must have been even more distraught than I realised, not to recognise my own nephew today. Inexplicable, inexcusable, really. But then these are unprecedented times.

Many of us have been so depressed for the last couple of days. This Passover week had started so excitingly. Jesus had continued to make his mark again on so many new people. Though, on the other hand, I know he had upset a few disreputable folk in the Temple precincts... causing a threat to law and order, some said. Which must have been the final straw for some of our priests who, shamefully, feeling their superiority threatened, had then plotted with the Romans to arrest him, manufacture a guilty verdict and crucify him, along with a couple of common criminals. All too appalling to recount, to be honest. Even when I summarise it all quickly.

So now, we, his closest followers, are probably still in danger too. Prudently, we have decided to lie low in an upper room in Jerusalem, hiding away for temporary safety, awaiting any developments, but hardly daring to anticipate anything positive. I have to say it's a febrile atmosphere there, swinging from fierce determination one minute to abject terror the next. But waverers have been uplifted in keeping the faith by many who remain convinced this isn't the end, somehow. The first massively encouraging sign perhaps being the empty tomb that Mary and a couple of others reported back to us about this morning, in wonder and a little confusion. Had she even actually seen him in the adjacent garden...risen? My original despair still struggled on, despite this new hope, but after what has just happened to me, perhaps I of all people should straightaway have given her the benefit of the doubt.

A friend and I sneaked out this afternoon to fetch a few things from my house in Emmaus, a couple of hours walk hence. Of course, on the journey we argued about the meaning of everything. What we should do. What we could expect. Heads down, our body language betrayed a lot about what was going on in our hearts and minds. All our grief and pain. Our normal senses completely numb. So, at first we hardly noticed a stranger who came up behind us. 'What are you discussing?' he politely enquired. 'The scandalous events in Jerusalem, of course,' I replied. 'You must be the only person round here not to have been involved,' I continued, in some disbelief, too disgusted even to look at him. How could I possibly have spoken and behaved like that, I now wonder? Anyway, I gave him a quick précis.

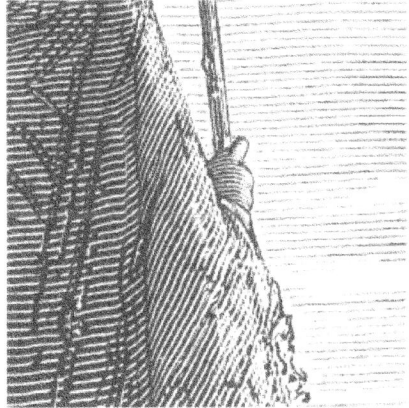

He was scathing. 'You are a fool. Don't you believe Moses or the prophets? About what had to happen.' And he went through the scriptures involving the promised Messiah. In some ways I resented his rebukes, but clearly he was strangely knowledgeable on the subject. Of course he would be, I now realise! Anyway, incredibly still not recognising him at the time, we wanted to hear more. He was compulsive listening. In due course, though he was planning to travel further than us, I persuaded him to come to my house for refreshments first.

I brought bread and wine to the table. And though it was really my duty to act as host, he insisted on taking the lead, giving thanks and breaking the bread. And as he passed it to me, I spied the nail marks in his hands. My heart seemed to stop for a few seconds. Surely not! How had we been so blind? We looked away in sheer embarrassment, even guilt, at our naivety. For a minute or so we remained thus transfixed, deep in thought and shame and incredulity. And when we looked up again, he had left. Gone, we knew not where.

My friend regained his voice first. 'Did not our hearts burn within us as we listened to all his teaching and explanations while we walked along the road? We can't stay here a moment longer. We must go back to Jerusalem immediately and tell the disciples and the others what we have heard and seen.' Not the end, we knew for sure now...because we had been witnesses to evidence of a miraculous new beginning.

The seven miles back from Emmaus took only half as long as usual!

Cleopas, the uncle of Jesus

Footnote

Many artists have felt compelled to depict the encounter and the humble supper scene, of its type second in popularity only to the iconic Last Supper itself...Rembrandt, Caravaggio, Durer, Tintoretto, Titian, Velasquez, Veronese.

As it was the gospel reading for Easter Monday in his time, Bach composed several special church cantatas.

Wounds...

It has been a terrible, terrible few days. Till now perhaps. Something astonishing may be happening.

By the middle of last week the figure of Jesus had never been more influential. Popular triumph beckoned. We all felt euphoric. Then apparent disaster. And since a traumatic weekend, everyone has even been wondering where his battered body might now be lying. Joseph of Arimathea's closely guarded burial sepulchre is mysteriously empty, so a few astounded women followers who visited it assure us all. I feel I must begin to think this all through again, for my own sanity.

Staggering me above all, though, is how God could have deliberately planned for such an excruciating death experience to happen. Had willed it so. All that physical, mental and spiritual torture. How could Jesus himself have been brought to accept and believe that such a cruel fate would be the path to success? Maybe he gave us disciples a few hints, but I don't think advance comprehension of such an extraordinary prospect could ever have sunk in to mere mortal minds, however much we trusted his every word. I need now to process a reassessment.

So again I go back a week or so. Rewind to that flamboyant joyful entry in noisy procession onto the Jerusalem Passover scene. Recall all that subsequent spectacular acclamation around the city. Then confront the contrast of that awful suffering on a barbaric cross.

Do I blame my colleague Judas? Partly. I think he was troubled by the envy and alarm Jesus had been creating in our Jewish authorities. He probably thought Jesus would be safer locked up until tempers had died down. Until the Romans too had stopped worrying about the tinderbox of civil unrest Jesus might be lighting. How could Judas have anticipated that fatal recriminations would develop so quickly and so disastrously? I understand his confusion. Before, during and after the arrest he helped to facilitate. What anguish he must be going through now. Suicide would not be a surprise.

Of course, the rest of us disciples let Jesus down too. Only an impulsive Peter tried especially hard to protect him in that nighttime garden of Gethsemane where he was arrested, but most of us quickly ran away into the dark night in fear for our own lives. Events then took their course behind the scenes. We could do nothing. Except feel wretched.

Eventually, to my bitter regret, I couldn't bear to watch the ensuing crucifixion ordeal for long, even from a distance. I am in awe that John and the womenfolk did so, close up. Subsequently, we have all been hanging around in Jerusalem in grief and further baffled impotence. Not sure what if anything Jesus had been expecting us to do next. As an example of our current frailty, Peter shamefacedly confessed to the rest of us cowards that he has three times had to deny even knowing Jesus. So here we are, gathered together, hiding in an upper room behind locked doors.

Actually, I am recounting events as if there is no hope. But yesterday the others told me about a miraculous moment. From nowhere Jesus appeared to them! His body was replete with the physical signs of his ordeal on the cross…nail marks in his hands, a gash in his side. Then he spoke to them. But I wasn't there at the time. So, heaven help me, I can't believe it really happened. Only if he comes again and lets me see, even touch, those sacred wounds, will I be able to credit the enormity of what might be unfolding. Only if I hear him speak my name…'Thomas…'.

Surely that won't happen? But it may. And, if it did, I pray it might make feeble me – wracked with my terrible doubt, totally undeserving – an everlasting example. Such that even the faintest of hearts can believe that Jesus's glorious resurrection and ascension is a reality. And a new world order, God's world order, is about to begin.

Thomas, a disciple of Jesus

Footnote

However deep our faith, there will be times of doubt when we can't sustain it under pressure. Something especially tragic, something way beyond the ordinary, something totally unexpected, something that feels unjust...all can rock us to our foundations.

Like Thomas, we might crave certainty, a proof to bolster us at a moment of weakness. No need to feel guilty. We are only human, after all.

YE CHOIRS OF NEW JERUSALEM...
Aftermath

Feasting and Fasting...

Shalom,

This is Reuben, with a cautionary open letter to any of my fellow Jews who are thinking of joining the followers of the teacher Jesus who was crucified a couple of generations ago. I worry that their growing community is not only attracting away Jews throughout the diaspora but also welcoming a lot of uncircumcised Gentiles. Many of our ancient rules and practices might be diluted in the years to come if it catches on. I'm not sure that those in the new movement will hold our Jewish customs to be sacrosanct, such that some might even be abandoned one day!

Let me inspire your loyalty with a few examples of our festivals pertaining to food. To see if I can remind you how precious they are to all ages.

The carnival atmosphere of Purim is always my children's favourite. All that dressing up to re-enact the story of Esther. All that booing, stamping, waving of our greggers every time Hamam's name comes up - it can't fail. And those delicious, three-cornered, sweet dough pastries, filled with poppyseeds and honey. Scrummy!

Of course, we also love our Hanukkah. Eight days of candle-lighting and rejoicing as a family. Singing special songs together, especially 'O fortress, rock', celebrating successive deliverances of our ancestors. Giving and receiving presents inevitably delights the children, along with playing their spinning-top game. Which brings me on to the food once more, and those lovely potato pancakes.

And, at agricultural New Year, when the farmers set aside a proportion of crops for priests and the poor - well, I find that is a good excuse to gorge on as many pomegranates and olives as I can lay my hands on.

I know I sound a bit of a glutton, but actually I do know the importance of fasting too - private and public. In my heart I will always cherish the memory of the fast before my wedding ceremony, expressing the beginning of a new stage of my life. Similarly, the fast before my first-born child.

Most notably for the whole community, following a long service in the synagogue on the eve, we all cherish the festival of Yom Kippur. A whole day without food or drink, helping everyone to concentrate on the spiritual, and the need for atonement and compassion.

Do you remember the story about a poor cobbler during one such occasion, muttering under his breath? 'I've done what I should on this special day, Lord. To be honest, my repentances are few. Some bad things I've wished to be visited on people who didn't pay me. Some working on the Sabbath when times were hard. Some unkosher food. But compared to you, Almighty, a nothing. You took my Rachel in childbirth, and the child also. You allow wars, pestilence, floods, disease, massacres, wickedness, everything. Listen, Almighty. How about this? I'll forgive you if you forgive me.' The rabbi had overheard him. A little later, once the single long blast of the shofar had signified the end of the fast, the two conferred. 'Did I do wrong, Rabbi?' came the worried question. 'Well,' began the reply. 'You were a little foolish. With a list like that, I'm disappointed you didn't ask God to forgive the whole town.'

Some of us, however, think it's best not to overdo the self criticism. There is another rabbi story about a rich man's son who 'has a bad attack of religion' and wants to be a saint. Always fasting and praying.

Dressing only in white. Drinking only water. Mortifying himself. Lying naked on the ground. Nails in his shoes. Whipping his back in penance. 'Look down in the yard,' says the father to him, 'at my white horse. Drinks water, nails in his shoes, rolls on the ground, whipped every day. Despite a lifetime of all that, he'll never become a saint!'

A lesson perhaps to avoid extremes of either sort. Of course, normally celebratory feasting holds the greater attraction for us all. But I very much doubt whether other nations and religions, even a new Jesus cult, could ever understand the full significance of fasting quite as well as we Jews do!

Shalom.

Reuben, a devout Jew

Footnote

The decades after Jesus's death were very confusing for most Jews. Should they support their traditional religious leaders? Or those who wished to retain his message within Judaism? Or join those who were widening their faith to embrace pagan Gentiles? All the time wondering whether Jesus would soon make his fervently anticipated return to herald earth's final judgement.

Set in our ways? Blind to new ideas? Resistant to change? Unwilling to listen to others? Stuck in a rut? Unable to grow or adapt? Scared of a challenge? In a comfort zone? Resting on our laurels? At some time in our lives, these accusations could be levelled at most of us.

But sometimes a good shakeup is just what we need. The wisdom is to retain the good and integrate it with the better. Finishing up with a new best.

...from your Valentinus...

Asterius here, jailer for many years in charge of a prison north of Rome. Responsible for locking up many miscreants on behalf of our Emperor Claudius. It's not a very edifying career, I freely admit. Gosh, the criminality and bestiality I have heard about and witnessed are legion, but, to be honest, not all of it is perpetuated by prisoners. The system itself is regrettably brutal too.

Actually, even some of our normal Roman customs leave me a little queasy. Take the festivities around the feast of Lupercalia in mid-February. Not content with sacrificing a goat and a dog, the priests then use strips of the animals' hides dipped in blood to whip women in the belief that it would make them more fertile. And the seasonal rituals may also include a sort of crude matchmaking session, with bachelors selecting the names of their next female targets via a lucky dip from an urn. Shows how much disrespect lies behind our typical attitudes to relationships between the sexes. Of course, our Emperor prefers all those men he needs as soldiers to remain unmarried and free from shackles. Maybe he also thinks they would otherwise lose some of the predatory virility needed for fighting? The norm, but all very unedifying.

In fact, there is only one man I have ever personally encountered of a totally different persuasion. A priest to that persecuted band of religious zealots...the Christians, still struggling on, 250 years after their hero died on one of our Roman crosses. In my jail, I'm afraid any Christian prisoners undergo terrible privations, maybe even worse than the others. I wish it could be otherwise but my job is always at stake. Surprisingly though, in time I did come to do everything I could to help Valentinus, that priest, to minister secretly to those benighted victims. He reassured them that they were cherished for their faithfulness to their God, even unto death. Some sort of life eternal would be their reward. And, partly because motivated by his example, but also by the following deeply personal story, here's how I finally came to completely change my own views on life and death. A very bitter sweet experience it all led to in the end, though.

Gradually, I had been becoming more and more impressed by that visiting priest. So much so, that one day I shared with him my deepest sorrow. At home, my daughter was going blind. All the healers and soothsayers to whom I had turned had proved helpless. But Valentinus just prayed with her. Called on his Saviour, Jesus, to restore her sight. And, miracle of miracles, it worked. Christians, count me in!

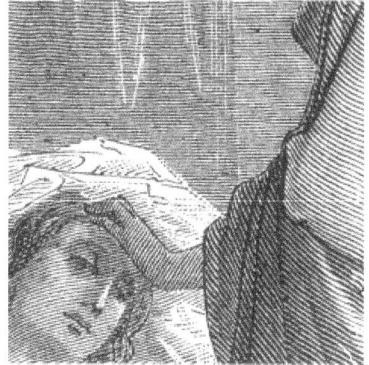

Just as impressively to me, along with his wonderful human empathies Valentinus also had no time for our society's acceptance of fornication or polygamy. Christians believe that marriage is a sacred communion between one man and one woman, lifelong. And, unlikely as it seems, the teaching had begun to appeal to quite a few regular Roman guys. Subversive. The authorities decided to stamp that out in the strictest way possible.

Probably you can guess the tragic outcome of all this. Yes, Valentinus was arrested. No way would he deny his actions or betray his beliefs. The ultimate punishment was inevitable. Firstly, they beat him almost senseless. Then they stoned him. And finally they decapitated him, displaying his severed head in public as a grim deterrent. And, irony of ironies, all in the middle of the Lupercalia season!

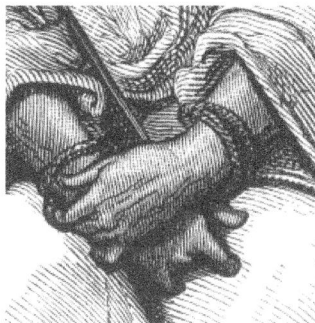

You can imagine how inconsolable was my daughter. But amazingly he hadn't forgotten her, despite his looming awful fate. Somehow he had arranged for a note to be smuggled to her, expressing his love and concern...and signed 'from your Valentinus'.

I compile this testimony in the probably vain hope that one day others will hear the full story of a true martyr. And wouldn't it be wonderful if in the future all men and women were inspired to send each other little notes and tokens of their love? Transforming Lupercalia into a sort of Valentinus' Day!

Asterius, a Roman jailer

Footnote

Initially disliked by many and viewed as just another Jewish heresy, the burgeoning Jesus movement faced only sporadic Roman intrusion. From its early support predominantly among the poor and downtrodden, it eventually spread into the middle and upper classes, with criticism of its perceived intransigence turning into respect for its probity and selflessness as it mellowed. The confusing dichotomy is exemplified in this dark story about Valentinus, with tragedy redeemed by love and devotion. However, before the Empire fell apart, the monotheistic message resisted a final burst of persecution and triumphed at the highest political and spiritual levels.

About the illustrator...

Paul Gustave Doré (1832-1883) was a child prodigy, first hired as a young teenager by a publisher in Paris. He was presented to Queen Victoria in 1873, who bought several of his large paintings for Windsor Castle. One of the most sought-after artists in nineteenth-century France, he was acclaimed mostly for his engravings and illustrations for books by Balzac, Rabelais, Milton, Byron, Cervantes, Hugo, Coleridge, Perrault, Shakespeare, Tennyson, Poe and Dante, along with 241 for the Bible.

Working with etched metal plates, he produced masterfully crafted images which were reproducible in mass quantities by the print shop. The originals took many hours of silent concentration to perfect, requiring thousands of finely detailed needle-fine lines to coalesce into intricate shape and shading. The effect is full of passion, energy and emotion.

About the Author...

Paul's family tree can be traced back over 600 years to North Yorkshire yeoman farmers near Northallerton. But in Victorian times one son moved to establish a branch in the Midlands, and Paul was born and raised in Birmingham, educated as a Foundation Scholar at King Edward's School, Edgbaston. Via Modern Languages at Pembroke College, Cambridge, he joined the sales department at the publisher William Collins, initially working in central London, then covering Oxford and Cambridge for a decade. His subsequent independent bookshop, the Book Castle, in Dunstable, Bedfordshire, prospered for a generation while also fronting his local publishing imprint, releasing well over 100 titles covering Bedfordshire, Buckinghamshire and Hertfordshire. He is President of the Dunstable and District local history society.

His parents and grandparents were staunch Methodists, but Paul has also been ecumenical, from Baptist to URC to Anglicanism, married for over 50 years to Ann, a Reader and lay minister. Now living in a village within easy reach of Cambridge, near most of their five children and nine grandchildren, he is enjoying worship at a wide variety of churches.

A selection of of highlights from

Book Castle
Publishing

Naked and You Clothed Me
A Spiritual Retrospective...
Ann Bowes

Spanning seven decades, tracing a life blending marriage and motherhood with Christian worship and service, evolving here against a backdrop theme of Ann's varied clothing choices along the way. Typifying how they might also shape and define any of us as we grow in them, work in them, play in them, sleep in them.

Clothes were certainly weaving a distinctive message into the fabric of her life as she moved from the Midlands via the Home Counties to Yorkshire - raising five children through her twenties and thirties, then moving back into work. Decades as a Church of England Reader underpinned her time as a hospital chaplain, then led to her founding and running a highly respected retreat centre in Bedfordshire for seven years. Eventually being licensed to a pioneering role as a lay minister to three rural parishes in North Yorkshire for a further seven years.

Supplementing the revealing autobiographical vignettes, with their line drawings and photographs, is a rich seam of over twenty of Ann's appropriately related Bible-based homilies.

'A store house of so many delights…your inspiring spiritual reflections provided me with much food for thought. Above all, your quirky sense of humour brings the whole account sparkling with life. A wonderful miscellany…a heart-warming read!'

'I thought I would dip into it before lights out! Two and a half hours later, I finally did…with more to read tonight. It is a page-turner.'

'It felt as if we were having a talk together…as if God was with us. I think it has changed my life.'

Book Castle
PUBLISHING

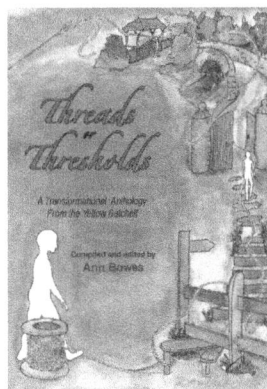

Threads
or
Thresholds
A Transformational Anthology...
Ann Bowes

Readers of Naked and You Clothed Me felt the book so echoed their own experiences that they wrote to share some similar pivotal moments in their lives. Threads being the clothes that sometimes defined or connected them; thresholds being the moments of challenge or transition.

Many contributors had encountered Ann in the context of her Christian example, empathetic teaching and pastoral care, over decades, for those of any faith or none. Gathered here under themes such as Identity, Community, Travel and Letting Go! In addition, Ann has supplemented this fascinating anthology, illustrated by line drawings throughout, with her own further reflections, musings, experiences and spiritual ponderings.

Here are a few typical reactions in response to Ann's autobiography that inspired the reactive contributions in this anthology...

'Your writing is wise, enlightened...a blessing to me.'

'How special - I read it too greedily and now want to reread it and taste every morsel...I love the warmth, humour, humanity and spirituality of your writing.'

'I love it because it chimes so very much with my own childhood. I look forward to reading a little each day before I go to sleep.'

'Your first-class wonderful book...I couldn't put it down. It made me laugh, cry...and has really helped and encouraged me so much.'

'Absolutely wonderful...It's been an amazing gift...I'm honoured to have read it...it has touched my soul.'

Book Castle
PUBLISHING

DUNSTABLE
with the PRIORY 1100-1550

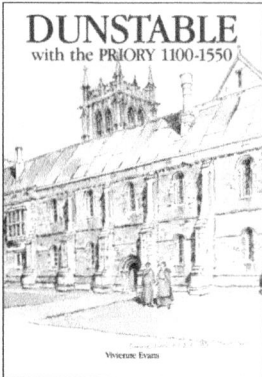

Dunstable
with the Priory
1100-1550
Vivienne Evans

Vivienne Evans

Henry 1's advisers planted a market town, of experienced businessmen, on the corner of his 'household manor', Houghton Regis. A royal palace was added and a few years later he invited a house of Augustinian canons from London to build a new Priory opposite. In due course a rival monastery, a Dominican Priory, was also established in the town. However, it took some years for everyone to work together and their struggle for supremacy was often stormy.

Throughout this period, Dunstable played an important role in national life - for example, its involvement in Magna Carta and the Peasants' Revolt. Nearly every king and queen of England stayed in the town, whilst the annulment in the Priory of Henry V111's marriage led to the foundation of the Anglican Church.

The town's site on the crossing of the famous Watling Street and Icknield Way was of crucial significance and fame. A commemorative cross was erected there to mark the nearby overnight resting place of the body of Edward 1's Queen Eleanor. And its strategic advantage facilitated Dunstable's rapid rise to be one of the country's most successful new towns.

A sequel covering the religious upheavals of the coaching era years of 1550-1700 is also available, Dunstable in Transition.

DUNSTABLE
in TRANSITION 1550-1700

Vivienne Evans MBE, the area's leading populariser of local history, delivered countless lectures, led many tourism initiatives and published a range of other books on Dunstable and the surrounding district.

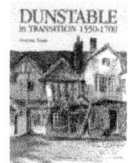

Book
Castle
PUBLISHING

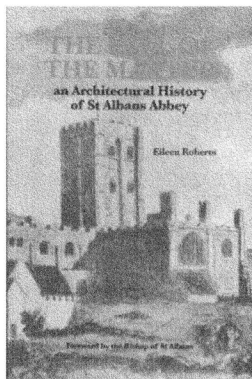

The Hill of the Martyr
An Architectural History of St Albans Abbey
Eileen Roberts

This popular but scholarly handbook covers the whole sweep of developments from the martyrdom of Alban to the relatively recent shrine restoration.

A chronological narrative describes and explains the origin and nature of each feature - whilst also telling of the many heroes and villains over the centuries, from the era of the Saxon Benedictine monastery, through medieval change, then on from near ruin to Victorian salvation and the abbey's subsequent glory and present role as cathedral for Hertfordshire and Bedfordshire.

The one hundred specially prepared pictures, plans and diagrams, plus a comprehensive bibliography and list of references along with a glossary, help give a rounded overview of the building's fascinating growth and challenges.

With art history degrees from three counties, long-term St Albans resident Dr Eileen Roberts lectured widely on architectural subjects and advised on the care of historic churches.

Book Castle PUBLISHING

Leafing through Literature

Writers' Lives in Hertfordshire and Bedfordshire

David Carroll

These neighbouring counties have had many close links over the years with some of the world's greatest writers. For example, John Bunyan spent all his life in and around Bedford, and George Bernard Shaw lived for nearly half a century at Ayot St Lawrence.

George Orwell, Beatrix Potter, Arnold Bennett and Charles Dickens are just some of the many other famous writers to be featured in this lively and entertaining book. But there are some less familiar ones too. Gascoigne of Cardington, for example, and Edward Young at Welwyn. However, from Sir Thomas More in the sixteenth century to Graham Greene who died in 1991, they all have one thing in common - a connection at some stage in their lives with Hertfordshire or Bedfordshire.

The author, David Carroll, has close family links with Hertfordshire, which eventually led to his compiling this book. He has written extensively, mainly on literary topics, for a wide range of regional and national publications.

Book Castle
PUBLISHING

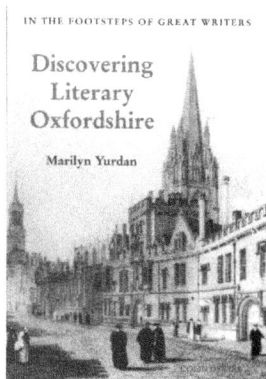

Discovering
Literary
Oxfordshire

Marilyn Yurdan

Discovering Literary Oxfordshire

Marilyn Yurdan

Authors, poets and playwrights in the county down the centuries. Associations began with one of the earliest examples of the Old English language, the Anglo Saxon Chronicles, part of which was written at Abingdon Abbey, and continued through the Middle Ages, Tudor and Stuart times, and the Georgian period.

Women are well represented, from Jane Austen's brief and unappreciated visit to the University onwards. Other female writers include Dorothy L Sayers, Vera Brittain, Winifred Holtby, Elizabeth Goudge, Nina Bowden, Antonia Fraser and Joanna Trollope.

Two favourite works in children's literature, Alice in Wonderland and Wind in the Willows, originated in Oxfordshire. A couple of writers achieved cult status, C S Lewis, especially in the States, and JRR Tolkien, whose Lord of the Rings trilogy was voted the Book of the Twentieth Century.

In all, information covers more than 100 writers of every genre from the classics to journalism, from local history to autobiography, from humour to the Aga saga. Many of them are modern.

In addition, a series of guided walks around central Oxford are outlined, showing where writers lived, studied, taught, worked and, in some cases, were buried.

'A treasure trove of information and fascination…a passport to the literary delights of Oxford and Oxfordshire.' from the Foreword by Colin Dexter.

Born in the city and studying there, before working as Assistant Custodian at the University's Sheldonian Theatre, Marilyn Yurdan has accordingly garnered many contacts to add weight to her specialism in writing numerous books about local history.

Book Castle
PUBLISHING

Exploring
History
All Around

Vivienne Evans

An illustrated guide, which is arranged as a series of seven thematic circular driving or cycling routes around most of Bedfordshire, plus north-east Buckinghamshire and north-west Hertfordshire, so perfect for family days out.

Packed with masses of corresponding background historical anecdotes and facts about all the relevant major towns and dozens of villages, it also equally lends itself to absorbing armchair reading.

'What a wealth of historical insight and knowledge she shares with us here. Add her immensely approachable style and it is easy to appreciate why she has been an inspiration for so many...Her style of broadcasting, lecturing and writing is so infectious and so well-informed...a certain joy to all who pick it up.' from the Foreword by John Pilgrim.

This detailed book is one of many valuable contributions to local literature by this enthusiastic lady, who was honoured for her tireless work in informing the public about and promoting interest in her counties of choice - for residents or visitors alike.

Book
Castle
PUBLISHING

Changes in our Landscape 1947-1992

Aspects of Bedfordshire, Buckinghamshire and the Chilterns

Eric Meadows

In the post-war years, this once quiet rural backwater between Oxford and Cambridge underwent massive growth and change - and the author's expert camera captured it all.

In his stunning, evocative and carefully composed photographs, we see an enormous variety of landscape, natural and man-made. Open downs and rolling farmland, woods and commons, ancient earthworks, moats and lakes, vanished elms, quarries and nature reserves. Building styles of all periods - churches, stately homes, pubs, bridges, town and village streetscapes.

Distilled from a vast collection of 25,000 photographs, this large-format book offers his annotated personal selection of over 350, in colour and monochrome, that typify the area through half a century of changes.

A Lutonian but educated at St Albans School, Eric Meadows' professional career as the leading local photographer of his day is secure. For over 40 years his work appeared in the Bedfordshire Magazine, in guides to Hertfordshire and Bedfordshire, in several of Pevsner's Buildings of England series, as well as on covers of Country Life and in numerous calendars.

Book Castle PUBLISHING

Journeys into Hertfordshire
foreword by The Marquess of Salisbury, Hatfield House

Journeys into Bedfordshire
foreword by The Marquess of Tavistock, Woburn Abbey

Journeys into Buckinghamshire
foreword by Sir Francis Dashwood Bt, West Wycombe Park

Anthony Mackay

These three landscape books of ink drawings reveal an intriguing historic heritage, and capture the spirit of England's predominantly rural heartland at the end of the twentieth century, ranging widely over cottages and stately homes, over bridges, streets, churches and mills, over sandy woods, chalk downs and watery river valleys.

Every corner has been explored in the search for his personally selected material, such that the resulting collection represents a truly unique record.

Brief notes and maps accompany the drawings to lend depth and to assist others in their searches around the counties.

Anthony Mackay's pen and ink drawings are of outstanding quality. An architectural graduate, he is equally at home whether depicting countryside or buildings. Often the medium he uses is better able to show both depth and detail than any photograph. As a result, many of his paintings, pastels and drawings have been exhibited publicly and been bought for private collections.

Book
Castle
PUBLISHING

Sinister...

He appointed me to be his Rock and I have failed. Tonight was the ultimate disaster. Some would say we Galilean peasants never stood much chance against the forbidding forces stacked against us...the Roman military, Pilate, Herod, the Chief Priest and his hypocritical brood of vipers. And yet...what hurts most is that one of us betrayed him and I couldn't prevent it.

Passover in Jerusalem is always such a precious week every year. And Jesus has certainly been making his charismatic presence felt here in the past few days. In unintended consequences, creating some danger for us all maybe. Today, with extra precautions over our safety, he planned a special supper for us disciples in an upstairs room. Unbeknown to the authorities, or so we all thought, but now I'm not so sure. Anyway, it was a notable occasion. Bonding. Enlightening.

He had been warning us for months not to worry about our relative status one to another, nor to vie for his attention, but I recall that there was nevertheless some initial jostling for a good position near him at the table. Personally, guilty as charged! In due course, after much fellowship, the climax to the meal came as the Lord symbolically gave up his body and blood in the bread and the wine. With a looming sense of dread, I feared this might be a farewell gesture to confirm the erstwhile hints that his life on earth would soon come to its end.

But the sequel was an even bigger shock. 'One of you will betray me,' he stated baldly, to the immediate consternation and rapid denials of everyone around the table. Even the guilty man disingenuously protested. Back at the start of the meal, I had instinctively seated myself on that felicitous 'dexter' (as the dreaded Romans term it!) side of the Lord - whilst on the 'sinister' side sat Judas Iscariot...the colleague, as I am now astonished to realise, who had secretly plotted and deceived everyone, including me. In my defence, it is regrettably true that Jesus alone ever knew the secrets of that disciple's heart. Challenged by the

Lord's gaze, the wretch's conscience couldn't sustain his pretence. And before anyone could stop him, Judas had darted away into the night. If I had my way, from henceforth that word for his position on Jesus's left would be forever associated with nefarious disrepute. Sinister.

Calmed and inspired subsequently at supper by Jesus's promises and resolve, the rest of us eventually accompanied him out to the Garden of Gethsemane for healing nighttime prayers. Though, once there, sadly most of us dozed off, leaving Jesus to meditate alone. A sacred occasion. Or thus was intended. But was Jesus by then mainly aware of an urgent need to prepare himself?

Abruptly, our peace was shattered by a shocking torchlit procession, too strong to resist. In a brutal denouement to the initial betrayal. A well-armed gang of rough soldiers, tasked with arresting the Lord, under the guidance of Judas at their forefront. A traitor's kiss was the sign. In a gesture far too late, I tried to retaliate forcefully. A futile act of bravery. Wholly insufficient to cancel out my growing sense of bitter self-recrimination. Surely I should long before have spotted the danger signs in our midst? No consolation in my despair to speculate that already Judas will be feeling even worse since that fatal action of his. I doubt that he can bear to live with himself from now on. Though, more importantly, whatever will the authorities do next with a captive Jesus? Distressingly, the Lord has predicted an imminent further dereliction of my duty towards him. Apparently, I am destined to deny three times ever having known him. Will I really be so craven? The very thought makes me ponder the long list of my previous inadequacies, not in the slightest softened via the benefit of any mitigating hindsight.

As for tonight at supper - no way did I merit that earlier seat on the Lord's right hand. Maybe the damned sinister side was actually what I too truly deserved?

Simon Peter, Cephas, a disciple of Jesus

An entry for a writing competition on this theme...Sinister